Run to You

Center Point
Large Print

Also by Rachel Gibson and available from Center Point Large Print:

Rescue Me

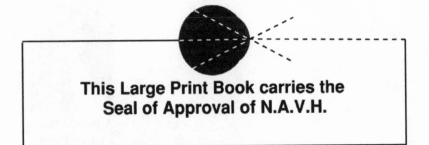

Run to You

Rachel
Gibson

CENTER POINT LARGE PRINT
THORNDIKE, MAINE

This Center Point Large Print edition is published
in the year 2013 by arrangement with Avon Books,
an imprint of HarperCollins Publishers.

The text of this Large Print edition is unabridged.
In other aspects, this book may vary
from the original edition.
Printed in the United States of America
on permanent paper.
Set in 16-point Times New Roman type.

ISBN: 978-1-61173-908-4

Library of Congress Cataloging-in-Publication Data

Gibson, Rachel.
Run to You / Rachel Gibson. — Center Point Large Print edition.
pages cm
ISBN 978-1-61173-908-4 (Library binding : alk. paper)
1. Man-woman relationships—Fiction. 2. Texas—Fiction.
   3. Large type books. I. Title.
PS3557.I2216R86 2013
813'.54—dc23

2013029140

For CC,
Claudia Cross,
my agent and advocate and friend.
Thanks for all you do for me.
You're the best,
RG

Acknowledgments

A special acknowledgment to my editor, Lucia Macro. Thanks for your patience and understanding. The space you gave me to breathe made this book possible.

Prologue

"Her name is Estella Immaculata Leon-Hollowell and she lives in Miami."

Vince Haven handed his good buddy, Blake Junger, a cold Lone Star, then took a seat behind his battered desk at the Gas and Go. "That's some name."

Blake took a drink and sat across from Vince. "According to Beau, she goes by Stella Leon."

Vince and Blake went back a long way. Blake had graduated BUD/S a year before Vince and they'd been deployed at the same time in Iraq and Afghanistan. While Vince had been forced to retire for medical reasons, Blake had served his full twenty.

Vince opened the folder on his desk and scanned the information that Blake's twin brother, Beau, had compiled for him. Beau had his own personal security business and had his fingers in a lot of different pies. He was one stealth dude and knew how to gather information that your average Joe couldn't access. He could also be trusted to keep all information strictly confidential.

Vince looked at a copy of a birth certificate, and there it was in black and white. His fiancée, Sadie Hollowell, had a sister she hadn't even known about until her father's death, two months ago. A twenty-eight-year-old sister born in Las Cruces, New Mexico. The mother and father listed: Marisol Jacinta Leon and Clive J. Hollowell.

"So, we think she knows Clive is dead." He moved the birth certificate aside to look over a color copy of a Florida driver's license.

"Yeah. She's been told. Told and didn't care."

That was cold but understandable. According to her license, Stella Leon was five feet, one inch and weighted one-fifteen. Which, knowing women as he did, Vince figured meant she was probably closer to one-twenty. She had black hair and blue eyes. He stared at the photo on the license, at the startling blue of her eyes set beneath dark brows. She was an exotic mix of dark and light. Hot and cool. Except for the color of her eyes, she looked nothing like Sadie, who resembled her blond beauty queen mother.

"She works as a . . ." He squinted and put his face closer to the paper to read Beau's handwritten scribbles. ". . . bartender at someplace called Ricky's. Her former careers include lead singer in a band, waitress, cashier, sales, and selling photographs to tourists." He sat back. "Busy girl." Especially since she didn't have to be. She had a big trust fund she drew money out of every month. He read further. Stella Leon had a police record for minor offenses and had lost a small claims lawsuit filed against her by a former landlord.

Vince closed the folder and reached for his beer.

He'd give the file to Sadie and let her make the next move. Get in touch with her long-lost sister or just let it go. Sometimes it was best not to tear off a scab. "What's your brother up to these days?" He took a drink, then added, "Besides ferreting out information."

"Usual shit." Blake and Beau were the sons of a former Navy SEAL, William T. Junger. Beau was the older of the two by five minutes, and while Blake had followed in his father's footsteps, Beau had chosen the Marine Corps. "Running his businesses and trying to stay out of trouble."

"Remember when we met up with Beau in Rome?" Whenever the twins drank too much, they always argued over who had the tougher training program, the Navy SEALs or the RECON Marines. Being a former Navy SEAL himself, Vince had his opinion, but he wouldn't want to have to prove it to Beau Junger.

"Barely. We were piss drunk."

"And got into a fistfight on the train." The brothers' arguments were notorious for being loud, relentless, and sometimes physical. If that happened, it was best just to get out of the way because as Vince had learned, if a guy tried to break up the fight, the Junger boys turned on the peacekeeper. They were two contentious peas from the same pod. Almost identical in every way. Two blond-haired all-American warriors. Iron-souled patriots who'd seen and done a lot and didn't know the word "quit." Vince took another drink. The kind of men a guy wanted at his side in a battle.

Blake laughed and leaned forward. "But get this, he says he's saving himself for marriage."

Vince choked on his beer. "What?" He wiped drops of beer from his chin. "You mean no sex?"

Blake shrugged one of his big shoulders. "Yeah."

"He's not a virgin." There were those who said that Vince had had a thing for easy women. Before he met Sadie, those people would have been right, but no one enjoyed down-with-it girls more than the Junger boys. There was even a wild rumor that the boys had hooked up with a pair of twins they'd met in Taiwan.

"Yeah, I pointed out to him that that particular horse had already left the barn, but he says he's going to remain celibate until he gets married."

"Does he have a woman in mind?"

"No."

"Had some sort of religious conversion?"

"No. He just said the last time he woke up with a woman he didn't know was the last time."

Vince understood that now. Since he'd fallen in love and all that good shit, he understood the difference between sex and sex with a woman he loved. Knew that with the one, the other was better. Knew that it became more than just an act. A need. More than just a physical release, but celibate? "He won't last," Vince predicted.

Blake raised the bottle to his lips. "He seems serious, and the good Lord knows once Beau gets something in his head, he's immovable."

Both the Junger boys were immovable. Loyal and stubborn to the core. Which made them good soldiers.

"He says it's been eight months."

"Eight *months?* And he hasn't gone bat-shit sideways?"

Blake set the empty bottle on the desk. "Some people think he was born bat-shit sideways." He chuckled and flashed the megawatt Junger grin that reached the corners of his eyes. "Me too." He pointed to the folder. "What are you going to do with that information?"

Vince didn't know. He'd have to talk it over with Sadie. Ultimately, it was her call on whether she wanted to contact her long-lost half sister. "Is this Beau's cell number?" He flipped open the file and pointed to the numbers scratched at the bottom of one of the pages.

"Yeah. He has several. Several cell numbers. Several business addresses and a secret lair near Vegas." Blake leaned back in his chair and crossed his arms over his chest. His brows lowered as if an unpleasant memory slid behind his gray eyes. There were guys who thought the Junger brothers had spooky eyes. Vince would say they were more hard, like steel, rather than spooky. The good Lord knew they all had hard memories, but just as quickly Blake's expression changed. He flashed his notorious grin, but this time it didn't quite reach his eyes. "So, when are you marrying that hot blonde of yours?"

Chapter One

Back Door Betty Night at Ricky's Rock 'N' Roll Saloon was always the second Thursday of the month. Back Door Betty Night was all about freedom of expression. A pageant of diversity that lured drag queens in from Key West to Biloxi. Lady Gay Gay and Him Kardashian competed for the Back Door crown with the likes of Devine Boxx and Anita Mann. The Back Door crown was one of the more prestigious crowns on the pageant circuit and the competition was always *fierce*.

Back Door Betty Night also meant the bartenders and cocktail waitresses had to dress accordingly and show more skin than usual. In Miami, where short and tight ruled the night, that meant practically naked.

"Lemon!" Stella Leon hollered over Kelly Clarkson's "Stronger" yowling from the bar's speakers. On stage, Kreme Delight did her best impersonation of a shimmering, leather-clad dominatrix. That was the thing about drag queens. They loved sparkles and glitter and girl-power songs. They were more girl than most girls, and loved girl drinks like appletinis and White Russians, but at the same time, they were men. Men didn't tend to order blender drinks. Stella, like most bartenders, hated making blender drinks. They took time and time was money.

"Lemon," a male bartender dressed in tiny white shorts and shimmer hollered back.

The Amy Winehouse bouffant pinned on the top of Stella's head stayed securely anchored as she raised a hand and caught the yellow fruit hurled at her. Around the base of the bouffant fastened to her head, she'd tied a red scarf to cover the many bobby pins holding it in place. On a normal night, her long hair was pulled up off her neck, but tonight she'd left it down and was hot as hell.

She sliced and squeezed and shook cocktail shakers two at a time. Her breasts jiggled inside her leopard-print bustier, but she wasn't worried about a wardrobe malfunction. The bustier was tight and she wasn't a very busty girl. If anything, she feared the bottom curves of her butt might show beneath her black leather booty shorts and invite comment. Or worse, a slap. Not that that was a huge fear tonight. Tonight the males in the bar weren't interested in *her* ass cheeks. The only person she had to worry about touching her butt was the owner himself. Everyone said Ricky was just "friendly." Yeah, a friendly pervert with fast hands. They also said he had mafia connections.

She didn't know if that was true, but he did have "associates" with names like Lefty Lou, Fat Fabian, and Cockeyed Phil. She definitely remained on high alert when Ricky was around. Lucky for her, he didn't usually show up until a few hours before closing, and Stella was usually long gone by three a.m. She wasn't the kind of person to hang out after her shift ended. She wasn't a big drinker, and if she had to be around drunks, she wanted to get paid.

"Stella!"

Stella glanced up from the martinis she set on a tray and smiled. "Anna!" Anna Conda was six feet of statuesque queen all wrapped up in reptilian pleather. Over the past few years, Stella had gotten to know several of the queens fairly well. As with everything in life, some of them she liked. Others, not so much. She genuinely liked Anna, but Anna was moody as hell. Her moods usually depended on her latest boyfriend. "What can I get you?"

"Snake Nuts, of course." The tips of her shiny green lips lilted upward. If it wasn't for Anna's deep voice and big Adam's apple, she might have been pretty enough to pass for a woman. "Put an umbrella in it, honey." Applause broke out as Kreme exited the stage, and Anna turned toward the crowd. "Have you seen Jimmy?"

Jimmy was Anna's leather daddy, although neither was exclusive. Stella grabbed a bottle of vodka, amaretto, and triple sec. "Not yet." She scooped ice into a shaker and added the alcohol and an ounce of lime juice. "He'll probably wander in." Stella glanced at the clock. It was after midnight. One more hour of competition before this month's Back Door Betty was crowned. While the stage was set for the next contestant, a mixed murmur of male voices filled the void left by the music. Besides the employees, few true females filled the bar. Although Back Door Betty Night tended to get loud, it never rose to the same level as a bar packed with real women.

Anna turned back toward Stella. "Your Amy eyeliner looks good."

Stella shook the cocktail, then poured it into a lowball glass. "Thanks. Ivana Cox did it for me." Stella was fairly competent when it came to makeup, but Amy Winehouse eyeliner was beyond her capabilities.

"Ivana's here? I hate that bitch," Anna said without rancor.

Last month she'd loved Ivana. Of course, that had been after more than a few Snake Nuts. "She did my eyebrows, too. With a thread." Stella grabbed a straw and a little pink umbrella and stuck them into the drink.

"Hallelujah. Thank God someone finally got rid of that unibrow." Anna pointed one green fingernail between Stella's eyes.

"It was painful."

Anna's hand fell to the bar and she said in her deep baritone voice, "Honey, until you tuck your banana in your ass crack, don't talk to me about pain."

Stella grimaced and handed Anna her drink. She didn't have a banana, but she did have an ass crack and she was positive she'd never purposely tuck anything in it. "Do you have an open tab?" She did wear thong underwear, but the string of a thong was nowhere near the size of a banana.

"Yeah."

Stella added the drink to Anna's already impressive bill. "Are you performing tonight?"

"Later. Are you?"

Stella shook her head then looked at the next drink order. House wine and a bottle of Bud. Easy. Sometimes, on a slow night, she took the stage and belted out a few songs. She used to sing in an all-girl band, Random Muse, but the band broke up when the drummer slept with the bass guitarist's boyfriend and the two girls duked it out on stage at the Kandy Kane Lounge in Orlando. Stranding her in Florida several years ago. She liked Florida and ended up staying.

She grabbed a bottle of white wine and poured it into a glass. Stella had never understood why women fought over a man. Or hit each other at all. High on her list of things never to do, right above tucking anything the size of a banana in her ass crack, was getting punched in the head. Call her a baby, but she didn't like pain.

"Break me off a piece of that."

Without looking up and with little interest, Stella asked, "Of what?"

"Of that guy who just came in. Standing next to the Elvis jumpsuit."

Stella glanced through the dimly lit bar to the white suit behind Plexiglas bolted to the wall across from her. Ricky claimed the suit had once belonged to Elvis, but Stella wouldn't be surprised to discover it was as big a fake as the signed Stevie Ray Vaughn Stratocaster above the bar. "The guy in the baseball cap?"

"Yeah. He reminds me of that G.I. Joe guy."

Stella reached into the refrigerator beneath the bar and grabbed a bottle of Bud Light. "What G.I. Joe guy?"

Anna turned back to Stella, and the light above the bar caught in the green glitter in her lashes. "The one in the movie. What's his name . . . ?" Anna raised a hand and snapped her fingers, careful not to snap off her green snakeskin nails. "Tatum . . . something."

"O'Neal?"

"That's a female." She sighed as if Stella was hopeless. "He was also in my all-time favorite movie, *Magic Mike*."

Stella frowned and grabbed a chilled glass. Of course Anna loved *Magic Mike*.

"I wanna bite him. He's yummy."

Stella glanced at the orders on the screen in front of her. She liked Anna, but the queen was a distraction. Distraction slowed her down. The bar was hopping, and slowing down cost money. "Magic Mike?"

"The guy next to the Elvis suit." A frown tugged at the corners of Anna's shiny green lips. "Military. I can tell just by the way he's leaning against the wall."

Stella removed the bottle cap and set it and the glass next to the wine on a tray. A waitress dressed as a zombie Hello Kitty whisked the tray away. Out of all the men in the bar, Stella wondered how Anna noticed the guy standing across the bar. He was dressed in black and blended into the shadows.

"He's straight. A real hard-ass," Anna answered as if she'd read Stella's mind. "And so on edge he's about to explode."

"You can tell all that from here?" Stella could hardly make out his outline as he leaned one shoulder into the lighter wood of the wall. She wouldn't have noticed him at all if Anna hadn't pointed him out. Just one more unsuspecting tourist who'd wandered in off the street. They didn't usually stay long once they figured out they were surrounded by queens and every other flavor of the rainbow.

Anna raised a hand and made a circle with her big palm. "It's in his aura. Straight. Hard-ass. Hot sexual repression." Her lips pursed around the straw and she took a sip of her drink. "Mmm."

Stella didn't believe in auras or any of the woo-woo psychic stuff. Her mother believed enough for both of them and her grandmother was a staunch woo-woo follower. Abuela was into miracles and Marian apparitions and claimed to have once seen the Virgin Mary on a taco chip. Unfortunately, Tio Jorge ate it before she could put it in a shrine.

"I think I'll go say hey. You'd be surprised how many straight men troll for queens."

Actually, she wouldn't. She'd worked at Ricky's too long to be surprised by much. Although that didn't mean she understood men. Gay or straight or anywhere in between. "Could be he is a tourist and just wandered in."

"Maybe, but if there's one bitch to turn a straight man, it's Anna Conda." Anna lowered her drink. "G.I. Joe needs to be thanked for his service, and I'm suddenly feeling patriotic."

Stella rolled her eyes and took an order from a heavyset man with a thick red beard. She poured the Guinness with a perfect head and was rewarded with a five-dollar tip. "Thank you," she said through a smile, and stuffed the bill into the small leather pouch tied around her hips. She had a tip jar, too, but she liked to empty it regularly. There had been too many times when drunks had helped themselves.

She glanced at Anna heading across the bar, blue and green lights blinking in her size thirteen acrylic heels with each step she took.

Roy Orbison's iconic "Pretty Woman" rocked the bar's speakers as Penny Ho strutted the short stage in thigh-high boots and blue-and-white hooker dress, looking remarkably like Julia Roberts. Apparently, "Pretty Woman" was popular among drag queens and tiara tots.

Over the next hour, Stella poured shots, pulled drafts, and gave the martini shakers a workout. By one-thirty, she'd changed out of her four-inch pumps and into her Doc Martens. Even with the thick cushion of the floor matting, her feet had not been able to hold out for more than six hours. Her old Doc boots were scuffed, but they were worn in, comfortable, and supported her feet.

After Penny Ho, Edith Moorehead took the stage and shimmied in a meat gown to Lady Gaga's "Born This Way." It just went without saying that the dress was an unfortunate choice for a big girl like Edith. Unfortunate and dangerous for the people who got hit with flying flank steak.

Stella fanned her face with a cardboard coaster as she poured a glass of merlot. She was off in half an hour and wanted to get her side work done before the next bartender took her place. In the entertainment district of Miami, bars were open 24/7. Ricky chose to close his between five and ten a.m. because business slowed during those hours, and due to operating costs, he lost money by staying open. And more than groping an unsuspecting female employee, Ricky loved money.

Stella lifted her long hair from the back of her neck and gazed across the bar. Her attention stopped on a couple in fairy wings going at it a few feet from the white Elvis suit. They'd better take it down a notch or one of the bouncers would bounce them. Ricky didn't tolerate excessive PDA or sex in his bar. Not because the man had even a passing acquaintance with anything resembling a moral compass, but because, gay or straight, it was bad for business.

Wedged between the fairy couple and the Elvis suit, Anna's G.I. Joe sat back farther in the shadows. A slash of light cut across his shoulder, wide neck, and chin. The strobe at the end of the stage flashed on his face, his cheeks, and the brim of his hat. By the set of his jaw, he didn't appear happy. A smile twisted a corner of Stella's lips and she shook her head. If the man didn't like queens and in-betweens, he could always leave. The fact that he still sat there, soaking in all the homosexual testosterone surrounding him, likely meant he had a case of "closet gay." Anger was a classic sign, at least that's what she'd heard from homosexual men who were free to be themselves.

After Edith, Anna hit the stage to Robyn's "Do You Know." Her lip-synching was spot-on. Her stage presence was good, but in the end, Kreme Delight won the night and the Back Door Betty crown. Anna stormed off the stage and out the front door. Stella glanced across the room toward the white Elvis suit. G.I. Joe was gone, too. Coincidence?

At one forty-five, she was caught up on most of her side work. She sliced fruit and restocked olives and cherries. She washed down the bar and unloaded the industrial-size dishwasher. At two, she closed out, transferred tabs, and stayed around long enough to get tipped out. She untied her leather tip purse from around her hips and stuffed it into a backpack along with her heels and hairbrush. Out of habit, she took out her Russian Red lipstick. Without a mirror, she applied a perfect swipe across her mouth. Some women liked mascara. Others rouge. Stella was a lipstick girl. Always red, and even though she'd been raised to believe only fast girls wore red, she never went anywhere without ruby-colored lips.

She fished the keys to her maroon PT Cruiser from the backpack. The car had more than one hundred thousand miles on it and needed new shocks and struts. Riding in it jarred the fillings from your teeth, but the air-conditioning worked and that was all Stella cared about.

She said good-bye to the other employees and headed out the back door. June, warm and slushy, pressed into her skin despite the early morning hour. Stella had been born and raised in Las Cruces and was used to some humidity, but summers in Miami were like living in a steam bath, and she'd never quite gotten used to how it lay on her skin and weighted her lungs. Occasionally, she thought about returning home. Then she'd remember why she left, and how much better she liked her life now.

"Little Stella Bella."

She glanced up as she shut the door behind her. Crap. Ricky. "Mr. De Luca."

"Are you leaving so soon?"

"My shift was over half an hour ago."

Ricardo De Luca was a good seven inches taller than Stella and easily outweighed her by a hundred pounds. He always wore traditional guayabera shirts. Sometimes zipped, sometimes buttoned, but always pastel. Tonight it looked like tangerine. "You don't have to leave so soon." His lifestyle had aged him beyond his fifty-three years. He might have been handsome, but too much booze made him pink and bloated. He had a black ponytail and soul patch because he was under the delusion that it made him look younger. It just made him look sad.

"Good night," she said, and stepped around him.

"Some of my friends are meeting me here." He grabbed her arm, and his booze-soaked breath smacked her across the face. "Party with us."

She took a step back but he didn't release her.

Her Mace was in her backpack, and she couldn't get to it one-handed. "I can't." Anxiety crept up her spine and sped up her heart. *Relax. Breathe,* she told herself before her anxiety turned into panic. She hadn't had a full-blown attack in several years. Not since she'd learned how to talk herself out of one. *This is Ricky. He wouldn't hurt you.* But if he tried, she knew how to hurt *him.* She really didn't want to shove the heel of her hand in his nose or her knee in his junk. She wanted to keep her job. "I'm meeting someone," she lied.

"Who? A man? I bet I have more to offer."

She needed her job. She made good money and was good at it. "Let go of my arm, please."

"Why are you always running away?" The lights from the back of the bar shone across the thin layer of sweat above his top lip. "What's your problem?"

"I don't have a problem, Mr. De Luca." And she pointed out rather reasonably, or so she thought, "I'm your employee. You're my boss. It's just not a good idea for us to party together." Then she topped it off with a little flattery. "I'm positive there are a lot of other women who would just love to party with you." She tried to pull away but his grasp tightened. Her keys fell to the ground, and an old familiar fear turned her muscles tight. *Ricky wouldn't hurt me,* she told herself again as she looked into his drunken gaze. He wouldn't hold her against her will.

"If you're nice to me, I'll be nice to you."

"Please let go." Instead, he gave her a hard jerk. She planted her free hand on his chest to keep from falling into him.

"Not yet."

A deep rasp of a voice spoke from behind Ricky. "That's twice." The voice was so chilly it almost cooled the air, and Stella tried in vain to look over Ricky's left shoulder. "Now let her go."

"Fuck off," Ricky said, and turned toward the voice. His grip slid to her wrist and she took a step back. "This is none of your business. Get out of my fucking lot."

"It's hot and I don't want to work up a sweat. I'll give you three seconds."

"I said fuc—" A solid thud snapped Ricky's head back. His grasp on her relaxed and he slid to the ground. Her mouth fell open and she sucked in a startled breath. Her Amy pouf tilted forward as she stared down at the tangerine lump at her feet. She blinked at him several times. What had just happened? Ricky looked like he was out cold. She pushed at his arm with the toe of her boot. Definitely out cold. "Holy frijole y guacamole," she said on a rush of exhaled breath. "You killed him."

"Not hardly."

Stella glanced up from Ricky's tangerine shirt to the big chest covered in a black T-shirt in front of her. Black pants, baseball cap, he was almost swallowed up in the black night like some hulking ninja. She couldn't see his eyes, but she felt his gaze on her face. As cool as his voice and just as direct. There was something familiar about him. "I don't think that was three seconds."

"I get impatient sometimes." He tilted his head to one side and glanced down at Ricky. "This is your boss?"

She looked down at Ricky. He *was* her boss. *Not now.* She couldn't work for him now, which was moot because she was pretty sure she was fired. "Is he going to be okay?" And that made her mad. She had rent and utilities and a car payment.

"Do you care?"

Ricky snored once, twice, and she glanced back up into the shadows beneath the brim of his hat. Square chin and jaw. Thick neck. Big shoulders. Anna's G.I. Joe. Did she care? Probably not as much as she should. "I don't want him to die."

"He's not going to die."

"How do you know?" She'd heard of people dying from one blow to the head.

"Because if I wanted him dead, he'd be dead. He wouldn't be snoring right now."

"Oh." She didn't know anything about the man standing in front of her, but she believed him. "Is Anna out here with you?" She looked behind him at the empty parking lot.

"Who?"

Stella knelt down and quickly grabbed her keys

by Ricky's shoulder. She didn't want to touch him, but she paused just long enough to wave her hand in front of his eyes to make sure he was good and truly out. "Ricky?" She peered closer looking for blood. "Mr. De Luca?"

"Who's Anna?"

"Anna Conda." She didn't see blood. Which was probably a good sign.

"I don't know any Anna Conda."

Ricky snored and blew his gross breath on her. She cringed and stood. "The drag queen in the snake gown. You're not out here with her?"

He folded his arms across his big chest and rocked back on his heels. The shadow from the brim of his hat brushed the bow of his scowling top lip. "Negative. There isn't anyone else out here." He pointed to her and then to the ground. "Except you and Numb Nuts."

Sometimes tourists wandered into the lot or parked in it illegally. What did a girl say to a guy who'd knocked out another guy on her behalf? No one had ever come to her defense like that before. "Thank you," she guessed.

"You're welcome."

Why had he? A stranger? G.I. Joe was big. A lot bigger than Ricky, and it didn't look like an ounce of fat would have the audacity to cling to any part of his body. She'd have to jump up to deliver a stunning nose jab or eye poke, and she suddenly felt small. "This is employee parking. What are you doing out here?" She took a step back and slid her pack off her shoulder. Without taking her eyes from his, she slid her finger to the zipper. She didn't want to Mace the guy. That seemed kind of rude, but she would. Mace him, then run like hell. She was pretty fast for a short girl. "You could get towed."

"I'm not going to hurt you, Stella."

That stopped her fingers and brought her up short. "Do I know you?"

"No. I'm here on behalf of a second party."

"Hold on." She held up a hand. "You've been out here waiting for me?"

"Yeah. It took you a while."

"Are you from a collection agency?" She glanced toward the front of the lot, and her PT Cruiser was still in its slot. She didn't have any other outstanding debts.

"No."

If he were going to serve her with a subpoena, he would have when he'd first walked into the bar. "Who is the 'second party' and what do they want?"

"I'll buy you coffee at the café around the corner and we'll talk about it."

"No thanks." She carefully stepped over her boss but kept her eyes on him just in case he woke and grabbed her leg. "Just tell me and let's get this over with." Although she could probably guess.

"A member of your family."

That's what she thought. She was so relieved not to feel Ricky's pervy hand on her leg, she relaxed a fraction. "Tell them I'm not interested."

"Ten minutes in the café." He dropped his hands to his sides and took several steps back. "That's it. And we should get moving before Numb Nuts comes around. I don't like to put a guy down twice in one night. Could cause brain damage."

What a humanitarian. Although she'd really rather not be around when Ricky woke up, either. Or when one of his sleazy "associates" rolled in. Or have G.I. Joe "put him down" again and cause brain damage. Or in Ricky's cause, *more* brain damage.

"And it will save us both the trouble of me knocking on your door tomorrow," he added.

He was as relentless as he looked, and she didn't doubt him. "Ten minutes." She'd rather hear what he had to say in a busy café than at her front door. "I'll give you ten minutes and then I want you to tell my family to leave me alone." Behind her, Ricky snorted and snored, and she looked back at him one last time as she moved toward the street.

"That's all it will take."

She walked beside him from the dark lot into the bright, crazy nightlife of Miami. Tubes of pink and purple neon lit up clubs and Art Deco hotels. Shiny cars with custom rims and booming systems thumped the pavement. Even at three in the morning, the party was still going strong.

"Maybe we should call an ambulance for Ricky," she said as they passed a drunk tourist puking on a neon-blue palm tree.

"He's not that hurt." He moved closest to the street as he dug into a side pocket of his pants.

"He's unconscious," she pointed out.

"Maybe he's a little hurt." He pulled out a cell and punched a few numbers on his phone. "I'm on a traceable. I need you to call Ricky's Rock 'N' Roll Saloon in Miami and tell them there's someone passed out on their back doorstep." He laughed as he took Stella's elbow and turned the corner. The commanding touch was so brief, it was over before she had time to pull away. So brief, yet it left a hot imprint even after he dropped his hand. "Yeah. I'm sure he's drunk." He laughed again. They moved to the curb and he stuck out his arm like a security gate as he looked up and down the street. "I'm headed there in about an hour. It should go down easy." Then he pointed at the café across the street as if he was in command. In charge. The boss.

No one was in charge of Stella. No one commanded her anymore. She was the boss. Not that it mattered. She'd give this guy ten minutes of her time and then it was sayonara, G.I. Joe.

Chapter Two

Stella plopped her backpack on the seat of a metal and vinyl chair at the little Cuban café tucked between restaurants and bars in Miami Beach. G.I. Joe pulled out a chair for her and waited for her to take a seat. "Thank you." Nice manners from the guy who'd just punched Ricky in the head? The two just didn't quite fit.

"You're welcome." He sat across from her, and her gaze landed on his chest. Hard muscles covered in a black T-shirt. This was Miami. Men didn't go to clubs dressed like ninjas or stunt doubles in an action movie. Not even on Back Door Betty Night. They wore cotton or linen button-down shirts tucked into designer jeans they probably couldn't afford. Even if they had to eat hot dogs every night, they dressed like jetsetters and ballers who had money to burn.

A waitress in a tiny pink T-shirt, smooth black ponytail, and big gold earrings set two menus on the table. "You back already?" she asked, her accent barely discernable.

"I've changed my mind about that flan." He reached for his hat and tossed it on the chair beside him. He looked up at the waitress, and Stella got her first good look at him. Like his muscles, his face looked hard, too. Hard like he'd been chiseled from stone. Like an action figure in an action movie come to life. "Black coffee." Captain America with a nasty case of hat hair.

The waitress turned her attention to Stella. "For you, miss?"

"I'll just have decaf." Caffeine was the last thing her central nervous system needed. As it was, she was going to be awake a long time anyway, trying to sort this night out in her head. "Cream and sugar."

Joe watched the waitress walk away and combed his fingers through his short blond hair. "What time do you have to meet your someone?" He glanced at the big watch on his wrist, then looked across the table at Stella. "Or was that a lie?"

Gray. His eyes were gray. The color of storm clouds and smoke. Anna Conda had said he looked like Channing Tatum, but Stella didn't really see it. Perhaps the shape of jaw and mouth was similar, but Joe was older than the *Magic Mike* star. Late thirties maybe, with tiny creases at the corners of his eyes. She couldn't imagine that he was a smiley guy. They were probably scowl lines. "What?"

"You told your boss you were meeting some-one."

Oh. "I just wanted him to let me go." She shook her head, and her Amy bouffant shifted. "How long were you out in the parking lot?"

"About twenty minutes." He sat back in his chair like he was irritated and folded his big arms across his bigger chest.

"Sorry." She reached above her head and untied the red scarf from her hair. "If I'd known I was being stalked, I would have hurried." She shoved the scarf in her pack, then started pulling out bobby pins.

"The laws of stalking vary from state to state, but generally they are defined as a person who repeatedly follows and harasses another person and poses a credible threat of physical harm, whether expressed or implied. Of course that's the short version." He paused a moment to watch her pull the pins from her hair before he added, "The key word is 'repeatedly.' Tonight is the first time I've seen you, so I think it's safe to say I'm not a stalker."

She didn't know if she should be alarmed that he knew the rules of stalking. Long or short version. She shoved a fistful of pins into her backpack, then pulled the bouffant from the top of her head and set it on the table. Instantly she felt cooler. "So what are you?" she asked, although she could guess. Stella wasn't exactly hiding from anyone, but she didn't make finding her as easy as a Google search. She'd never been involved in any sort of social media and mostly used the Internet to look up drink recipes and YouTube videos. "Are you a private investigator?" She ran her fingers through her hair, from the top of her forehead to her crown.

His stormy-colored gaze moved from her face to the bouffant on the table. "No. Private security."

"Like a bodyguard?" He looked like he could be a bodyguard.

"Among other things." The waitress returned with two cups of coffee and a small plate with flan drizzled in caramel.

"What other things?"

He waited until the waitress walked away before he answered, "Things you don't need to know about."

"Secret spy things?"

He picked up his fork and pointed to the wig. "What is that?"

The subject of secret spy things apparently not a topic for conversation, she answered, "A hairpiece."

"It looks like one of those yappy dogs." He paused to cut into his dessert. "Like a fat Pekingese."

Out of everything that had happened that night, he wanted to judge her Amy bouffant? She poured a splash of cream into her coffee and added a packet of sugar. "So, who paid you to look for me?" She stirred, and with her free hand, she reached behind her neck and pulled her hair over one shoulder. The fine black strands brushed the top of her bustier and curled beneath the curve of her left breast. She thought about her family and wondered which one had actually coughed up their own money to find her. It wasn't her mother. Her mother knew where she lived, but Stella doubted Marisol had told anyone. Not because she was tight-lipped, but because Stella had made her mother swear secrecy on the life of baby Jesus. And swearing on baby Jesus was deadly business. Her first guess would be her mother's ex-husband. "Carlos?" Although she couldn't imagine what he'd want from her these days. *Money.* Her biological father had died recently and Carlos had to think she'd received some money. She hadn't. Her mother would have mentioned money.

He shoveled a piece of flan into his mouth, then raised the solid white mug and washed it down. "No."

She took a drink of her own coffee, then wiped off the smudge of red lipstick with her thumb. "Tio Jorge?" She liked her uncle Jorge. He was one of the few people in her family she wouldn't mind seeing. He'd always been good to her, but she couldn't imagine Jorge parting with a dime to find her. He was a good man, but an extreme tightwad.

He pointed the mug at her. "Your sister."

Equal parts relief and amusement curved her lips into a smile and she chuckled. "You've got the wrong girl." He'd hung out with drag queens, waited in a parking lot until two-thirty in the morning, and knocked Ricky out. For nothing. "I don't have a sister. Tons of cousins, but no sister." Thinking of Anna Conda and her interest in Joe's sexual aura turned Stella's chuckle to laughter. She placed her elbows on the table and laced her fingers together beneath her chin. "Maybe you should think of a new line of work."

His gray eyes stared into hers from across the table as he took another drink of coffee. Nothing registered on his face, as if the mere possibility of a mistake was so absurd it wasn't worth the effort of a single thought or expression.

"Whoever paid you is going to want her money back. I hope it wasn't much." She needed to get going. It wasn't her style to bullshit with strangers. She had to do a lot of that at work and preferred not to on her own time. There was nothing to keep her here now, except a perverse desire to see if she could get a reaction out of Mr. Stone Cold. "This stealthy ninja, lurking-in-the-shadows gig isn't working for you." And to be extra helpful she added, "I don't know what they taught you at your security school, but the next time you're working undercover at a drag queen pageant, you might think about blending in. Maybe wear some leather chaps or at the very least . . . pastel." The thought of him in assless chaps or a pink shirt with maybe a scarf cracked her up.

Too bad he didn't have a sense of humor. "I'm

not undercover, and your name is Stella Leon. Correct?" Without breaking so much as a smile, he picked up his fork and shoved more flan into his mouth.

He knew her name. She didn't know his but didn't ask. First, because she didn't care. And second, if he told her he might think he had to kill her. She tried and failed to control her laughter. God, she was funny sometimes. Maybe she should try stand-up comedy as her next career. She'd tried just about everything else. "Yep."

"Your sister, Sadie Hollowell, is looking for you."

Her laughter died and everything within her stilled. Shut down and off. Her heart. Her breath. The blood in her veins. Her hands fell to the table and she unlocked her fingers. "Sadie?" The name sounded odd coming from her mouth. She never talked about Sadie out loud anymore. Tried not to think about her and was for the most part successful. She pressed her palms and fingertips into the hard tabletop as if she could hang on to the smooth surface as her world tilted. "You know her?"

He shook his head and said between bites, "Never met her. I know her fiancé, Vince. He contacted me."

"Why . . ." Her voice cracked and she cleared her throat. Obviously, Sadie was just like her father. Hiring someone else to deal with a problem. "Why didn't she contact you?"

"Don't know. I'm sure she has her reason."

Her stilled heart gave a painful thump and lifted in her chest. A high-pitched buzzing started in the center of her head and moved to her ears. Stella knew the reason. The Hollowells had always hired someone to take care of their dirty work. Her. "What does she want?"

He took a drink of his coffee and looked at her over the top of the heavy mug. His gray gaze studied her as he slowly set it on the table. "Are you going to faint?"

"No." Maybe. Most definitely have a panic attack if she didn't remember to breathe, though. She pulled air into her lungs and slowly let it out like she'd been taught. She resisted her body's natural urge to pull shallow gulping breaths into her lungs as if she was drowning. "What does she want?"

"To talk to you."

"About what?" She probably wanted to make sure Stella stayed away. Away from the ranch and Sadie's inheritance, but Sadie didn't need to worry. Stella got the message a long time ago that she was not welcome in the state of Texas. Her anxiety leaked out of her toes and she tapped her feet.

"I don't know."

"Why? Why after all these years?"

"Now that is a question that I do know the answer to." He dug into his flan again. Far more interested in his dessert than in her. "She didn't know about you until her father died last month."

Her feet stopped. "What?" That wasn't possible. Could that be possible? Stella had always known about the sister she'd never met. The older blond sister who got to live with their father in Texas. The girl who lived on the JH Ranch and raised calves and won 4–H ribbons. The debutante who wore a white gown and long white gloves and got her picture taken for the newspaper. "How could she not know?"

"That's what I was told." He shrugged and raised the fork. "She didn't know about you until after your father died."

Clive Hollowell had never been her father. She remembered seeing him only five times in her life. He'd just been the man who'd accidentally knocked up her mother and set up a trust fund to take care of his mistake. Carlos had never been a father, either. He'd just been the man who'd moved in and lived off the Hollowell money like some people in her family.

She pulled her hands into her lap and stared at her blunt nails painted black. What did Sadie want to talk to her about? What could they possibly have to say to each other? Their father had loved Sadie. Sadie was the golden-haired golden girl. Stella was the dark-haired dirty secret.

"Sadie would like to know if you are open to speaking with her. She'd like to contact you."

"I don't—" She lifted a hand and dropped it back into her lap. Old feelings of rejection and the ache of wanting tumbled in her stomach and tangled around her heart. Emotions she thought she'd buried long ago. "On the phone?"

"Yes."

Her sister wanted to call her. She didn't know how she felt about that. Part of her wanted to tell her sister to go to hell and stay out of her life. The other part wanted . . . What? To at long last hear her sister's voice? "I don't know." She forced herself to look up at the man across the table from her. She didn't know him. Didn't even know his name, and yet he'd turned her world sideways and she felt like she was sliding off. "Does she want me to give you my phone number?"

"I have your number." He set his fork on the empty plate and drained his coffee. "I know your work schedule, driver's license and car tag numbers. How many parking, speeding, and various moving violation tickets you've had in the past ten years. I know how many times you've appeared in court, and your last four known addresses." He set the mug on the table and reached for his hat. "I know all that without really digging too deep . . ."

"How?"

He adjusted the hat on his head a few times. "Stealthy ninja secrets I learned in security school." He stood and pulled out his wallet. "Call the middle number when you make up your mind. Leave a message and I'll let Sadie know your decision." He slid a business card toward her, then threw money on the table.

She didn't know what to do. "What if . . ." She shook her head. She would not voice her deepest fear. Not even to herself. Especially not to this hard-eyed stranger.

"Talk to your sister. Don't talk to her. I don't care one way or the other. I told Vince I'd find you and I did. Once I hear from you, I'm out of it." Then he walked away, and she raised her gaze to his broad shoulders. Within a few long strides, he moved out the front doors and disappeared into the darkness.

Stella lifted a hand from her lap and picked up the card. Black, of course, with bold silver print. "Junger Security and Logistics Inc." appeared in the middle of the card with three numbers below: office, cell, and fax. She pressed the pad of her thumb into the card's sharp corner. She concentrated on the pressure and pinpoint sting. It was too much. Tonight had been too much. Ricky's slimy antics and Joe punching Ricky in the head. She didn't have a job now, and she didn't know when she would get another. Oh, she could probably sling drinks in a dive bar, but the tips weren't as good as in South Beach. If she didn't hurry and get a job, she'd lose her tiny apartment. True, it wasn't much, but it was currently home. There was money in her trust fund account from Clive Hollowell, but that money had never been hers and had always caused more problems than it had solved.

She took a deep breath and placed a hand on her bare throat. Too much. Tonight was way too much to handle. Ricky. Her job.

Sadie. Did she dare open that door?

"Can I get you anything else," the waitress asked as she took the empty plate and mug from across the table.

"No. Thank you." Stella grabbed her Amy bouffant and stuffed it in her backpack. She rose and looked at the card in her hand. If she left it on the table, the choice would end right now. She wouldn't have to think about it. She wished she could talk to her mother. Not that Marisol gave good advice, but sometimes it helped Stella to talk about things out loud. Sometimes she needed to vocalize her options and possible outcomes to get it all straight in her own head.

The strap of her backpack slid across her shoulder and she shoved the card into an outside pocket. It was twelve-thirty in New Mexico, and talking to her mother was not one of her options.

She left the café and headed back toward Ricky's. The wind had kicked up, and she ducked her head against the damp air. The first splashes of rain hit her bare shoulders and forehead and picked up as she turned the corner. From across the street, she paused to peer into the parking lot. Except for employee vehicles, it was empty. No prone body by the back door. No ambulance. No one lurking in the dark. Droplets pelted her face as she ran to her PT Cruiser and dived inside. With her heart pounding in her head for the second time that night, she started the car and sped out of the parking lot. Half a block from the bar, she flipped on the lights and wipers and headed toward her apartment near Fifty-eighth and Sixth. She glanced in the rearview mirror, half expecting someone to follow her. Something to happen. She wasn't exactly sure what, but it wasn't until she'd exited the Julia Tuttle Causeway that she started to breathe a little easier. She continued through the glittering lights of the high-rise buildings of midtown and under swaying traffic signals. Fifteen minutes later, she pulled into the assigned parking spot of her terra-cotta and red stucco apartment complex. She bolted from the car to the front of the building and up the stairs to the third floor. Once inside, she locked, dead bolted, and chained the door behind her. A light in the stove lit up a small part of the tiny kitchen. She paid eight hundred dollars a month for the six-hundred-square-foot apartment. Sparse IKEA furniture filled the space. A couch, two chairs, coffee table, and bedroom set. That was about it. She moved a lot and it made sense not to have a lot of possessions.

Stella walked into the kitchen and set her backpack on the counter. She grabbed a bottle of water and moved through the darkness to her bedroom. Exhaustion weighted her shoulders even as her mind raced. She flipped on the light and pulled a tank top out of a six-drawer oak dresser.

On a normal night, she might decompress in front of the television. Tonight it would take more than old reruns and infomercials. She unlaced and stepped out of her boots, then her bustier, leather shorts, and lace thong hit the bedroom floor. She moved into the bathroom, jumped in the shower, and washed the smell of Ricky's from her hair. As the water poured over the crown of her head, she let herself think of what it might be like to meet her sister. If it was true, and Sadie hadn't known about Stella, maybe they should meet. It couldn't hurt. Except . . .

Sadie was so successful. She'd gone to UT Austin and UC Berkeley and was a real estate agent in Phoenix. A top seller, or at least she had been before her father's death. Now she owned the JH Ranch and had a fiancé who loved her enough to hire G.I. Joe to track Stella down.

She turned off the water and wrapped her hair in a fluffy blue towel. Okay, so she might have occasionally plugged her sister's name into a search engine on the Internet. She might have kept up on her from time to time. When she'd been a kid, she might have read about Sadie in the *Amarillo Globe*, and she might have harbored a few vague fantasies about a sister reunion. Where they fell on each other's necks and wept for joy. Maybe they wore matching sister lockets and painted their fingernails pink because red was for fast girls. Perhaps they'd call and write and spend holidays with each other.

But that reunion never happened and she'd given up on those fantasies a long time ago. Fantasies were foolish and cost a big emotional price.

A second blue towel hung on the rack and she grabbed it. She dried herself and brushed her long wet hair. Sadie was five years older than Stella. Sadie was golden and successful, and Stella . . .

Wasn't.

She pulled on a pair of pink panties and a tank top. Sadie's mother had been a beauty queen from a respected family. Stella's mother had been a nanny from a long line of undocumented workers. One time when Stella had been about ten, she'd thought it would be funny to run into her mother's house and yell, "*La Migra! La Migra! La Migra!*" She'd never seen her stepfather or uncles move so fast. Especially Jorge, who'd bailed out the window. When everyone realized the border patrol wasn't really coming, she'd gotten in big trouble. In retrospect, she understood that maybe it wasn't the best of jokes.

She crawled into bed and nestled into her feather pillows. Even as a kid, no one thought she was as hysterical as she did. G.I. Joe hadn't thought she was funny. If she ever did meet Sadie, her sister probably wouldn't think she was funny, either. Or maybe, just maybe, her sister would share her sense of humor. It had to come from somewhere.

Stella turned on the television across the room. She found a *Two and a Half Men* rerun with Charlie Sheen before his "winning" and "tiger's blood" antics. She was positive she wouldn't fall asleep for a long time and was surprised when she opened her eyes later and sunlight spilled into her bedroom. On the tube, Jerry Springer acted like he gave a damn about the two women beating the crap out of each other over some redneck. She turned off the television and looked at the clock. It was a little after nine a.m. She had slept for only five hours, and she turned on her back and tried to go back to sleep. Her eyes drifted closed but flew back open as someone pounded on her door.

She lay still. Maybe it wasn't her door. *Bam, bam, bam.* Yep, it was her door, but it couldn't be the property manager. She'd paid her rent on time. If she didn't answer, the person would go away. She closed her eyes, but the pounding continued.

"Crap." She sat up and swung her legs over the side of the bed. It was probably Malika, her friend from work, and she stood and moved across the room to her closet. She reached inside and pulled out her short red kimono robe. She was certain everyone had heard about Ricky by now, and she was sure Malika would want the details.

Although Malika really should have called first, Stella tied the red belt around her waist and walked down the short hall. The closer she got to the door, the more she realized that Malika wouldn't pound so hard. One of the things she didn't like about her apartment, aside from the cheap carpet, was that there was no peephole in the door.

"Who is it?" she called out.

"Lou Gallo."

"Who?"

"Ricky De Luca's associate."

Crap! Lefty Lou. Ricky's friend with the thin black comb-over and missing left thumb. "What do you want?"

"Just a word," a new voice provided. Probably Ricky's other friend. The square one. The one as wide as he was tall. Fat Fabian. "One question and then we're gone."

"Just one?"

"Yeah."

She didn't believe them and left the safety chain on as she opened the door a crack. "What's your question?"

"Where's your boyfriend?"

"What boyfriend?" Through the crack she could

make out Lou's tropical guayabera and his sweaty neck.

"The one who hit Ricky last night."

"He isn't my boyfriend. I never saw him before."

"Right," Fat Fabian scoffed. "Who was he? Give us a name and we'll go on our way."

"I don't know his name." She had his card. She could give it to them and they might leave her alone. She'd be off the hook, but she didn't want to do that. She didn't know Joe, but she did feel a smidge of gratitude toward the guy. Although there might have been a better option than knocking Ricky out.

"Ricky wants you to come to the bar."

"Okay." She had no intention of ever going anywhere near Ricky De Luca. "I'll get dressed and drive over."

"No. You come with us now."

Not going to happen. "Sorry. Can't do that, boys. I have to dress and shower."

One thumbless hand reached through the opening and grabbed the chain. Stella gasped and her eyes widened as he pulled on it hard, once, twice. It all happened so fast and one of the screws popped halfway out of the wall. Pure adrenaline rushed across Stella's skin and up her spine and she slammed the door on his hand.

"Fuck!"

She opened it just enough to slam it again.

"Awww! Fuck!"

This time when she opened it, he pulled his hand back just in time. The door slammed closed and she dead bolted it before they could ram a shoulder into it. Which they did.

"I'm calling the police!" she called out.

The thumping stopped. "You can't stay in there forever."

"I'm getting my phone!" She moved to the kitchen and unzipped the front pocket of her backpack. She reached inside and pulled out the phone. G.I. Joe's card came out at the same time and she walked back across the room and put her ear to the door. She didn't hear anything, but that didn't mean that she believed for one second they would leave and never come back. Especially since she'd slammed Lefty Lou's hand in the door. Twice.

She was screwed. First by Ricky. Then Joe. Now Lou and Fabian. Men sucked. She'd never known one of them she could depend on. Except maybe Uncle Jorge, but he had ten of his own kids to worry about.

The cheap shag carpet scratched her feet as she moved to the sliding glass door leading to her balcony and looked out the vertical blinds. The two goons stood in the parking lot talking on their own cell phones. What was she going to do now? How long would she have to wait them out? Ricky's buddies couldn't stay out there forever. If they didn't leave soon, she would have to call the police.

The card in her palm stuck her finger and she opened her hand. At the moment, she had more pressing concerns than a reunion with Sadie. She looked at the bottom of the card and dialed the ten numbers with her thumb.

"You reached me," spoke the deep familiar voice. "Leave a message."

"Hello. This is Stella Leon." Just in case he didn't remember her she added, "Sadie Hollowell's sister. Listen, I just wanted to let you know that I won't be calling to set up a meeting with Sadie anytime soon." Once again, she looked through the blinds covering the door. "Ricky De Luca, my former boss, isn't real happy about you punching him in the head and sent his associates over here." She turned from the blinds. "They're camped out in my parking lot, but as soon as they leave, I'm going to leave town for a while." Where she was going, she didn't know. "So now isn't a real good time for a family reunion." She pushed end and set the phone on the kitchen counter.

She moved into her bedroom and pulled a big duffel from her closet. She'd wait for a few hours. If they were still camped outside after dark, she'd have to call the cops, but she really didn't want to call the Miami PD. She didn't want to file a report. They'd ask her questions she didn't know the answers to; she'd prefer not to make Ricky and his friends any madder than they were already.

She dumped underwear and bras into the bag. Maybe she'd be gone for a week. Surely that was long enough. She'd stay at a hotel and look for a job. Maybe in Orlando.

Next, she shoved shorts, tank tops, and two sundresses into the duffel. Makeup and hair products were followed by flip-flops and her iPad loaded up with about a thousand of her favorite songs. Everything from Regina Spektor to Johnny Cash.

She pulled on a blue ombré halter dress and her Docs. In case she had to run, she needed her good solid shoes. Her hair, she slicked back into a ponytail to keep it out of her face.

From the kitchen, her phone rang, and she walked into the hallway toward the sound. She didn't recognize the number coming across but was fairly sure it had to be Ricky. She thought about not answering, but perhaps she could defuse the situation and convince him to leave her alone. "Yes."

"Where are you?"

It wasn't Ricky. "Who is this?"

"Beau Junger."

Joe's name was Beau? Didn't seem to really fit him. It wasn't hard enough. He looked more like a Buck or Duke or Rocky. "I'm in my apartment."

"Are the Gallo brothers outside your apartment?"

She peered out the slice in the blinds. "I don't think they're brothers."

"One short and fat? The other tall and skinny?"

"Yeah."

"They're brothers. Do you see their beige Lexus LS?"

How did he know that? "Yes."

"Where is the vehicle oriented to your front door?"

"Several rows back and to the left."

"Okay. Do you have a bag packed?"

"Yes. I'm waiting for them to leave so I can run to my car."

"Forget your car. I'm still about an hour out. So at"—he paused as if looking at his big watch—"fourteen hundred hours, you're going to hear a commotion. Grab your bag and haul your ass out of your apartment."

"What kind of commotion? How will I know it's you?"

She wasn't sure, but he might have chuckled. "You'll know. There will be a black SUV parked at the curb closest to your unit. Get in."

"Your SUV?"

"Yes," he said, and the line went dead.

"Wait. Come back. What time is fourteen hundred hours?"

Chapter Three

Commotion. Stella considered a heated argument a commotion. Loud music was a commotion. Evidently, Beau Junger had a different definition. One that included a boom and black smoke and chaotic flashes of light. At the first sign of "commotion," Stella grabbed her bag, locked her door behind her, and hauled ass down the stairs as he'd directed. As she hit the ground floor, she glanced across the parking lot at the smoke pouring from beneath the Gallo brothers' Lexus. Amid the confusion of crackling light and blaring car alarm, a black Escalade pulled up to the curb. With her backpack across one shoulder and her duffel clutched to her chest, Stella yanked open the door and jumped inside.

"Holy frijole y guacamole!"

From across the big SUV, Beau Junger, aka G.I. Joe, aka Captain America, looked back at her through the lenses of his mirrored sunglasses. "Good afternoon." All calm and cool, he eased his foot off the brake, and the Cadillac pulled away from the curb. No squealing tires or racing engines or hail of bullets. Just cool air-conditioning, soft leather, and tinted windows.

"What did you do?" She looked back through the seats toward the billowing black smoke and the Gallo brothers yelling and pointing at their Lexus. "Did you blow up the Gallos' car?"

"Of course not. That would be against the law."

"And that isn't?"

"That's just a little flashbang." He took a deep breath. "God, I love the smell of flashbang."

All she could smell was leather and some sort of man soap. Like he'd scrubbed his face with Axe or Irish Spring or Lava. She shoved her duffel in the seat behind, and her forearm brushed his solid shoulder. "Little?"

He shrugged and pulled out of the apartment complex. "I've used bigger."

She didn't doubt it and turned forward. He struck her as a secretive kind of guy, and she knew better than to even ask where one might get his hands on a "flashbang." She wouldn't mind having at least one of her own. "Where we going?"

"Out of town." He glanced across the car at her. His sunglasses hid his eyes, but she could feel his gaze on her face. "Initially, I didn't gather intel on your boss. There was no need, but after our meet and greet in the parking lot, I've done a little digging." He turned his attention back to the street and pulled onto the 112.

She clicked her seat belt across her lap and dug her sunglasses out of her backpack. "What did you find out?"

"Ricky De Luca is associated with the mafia out

of Newark." He looked across his left shoulder and merged in front of a BMW. He named the family but it meant nothing to Stella.

"He's in the mafia? No way!" She shoved her big black sunglasses on her face and set the pack between her feet. "I thought that was just a rumor because he's Italian." Being Italian didn't mean he was in the mob any more than being Hispanic meant she loved tacos. Although she totally did. "I bet you're sorry you punched a mobster in the head."

"Not at all. Even if I'd had more information on him, I would have punched his head. And technically, he's not a member of the family. They launder money through his club, and in return Ricky gets protection from the Russian mafia."

"There's a Russian mafia, too?"

"Sure. There's the Italians, Mexicans, and Russians all running drugs, prostitution, and extortion in south Florida." He glanced at the GPS, punched a few buttons, and the screen changed. "The Gallo boys are soldiers for the Italians. They're in the mob."

Stella gasped and looked from Beau's long fingers fiddling with the GPS to his hard profile. "I smashed a mobster's bad hand in my door." The image of that thumbless hand grabbing and pulling the chain like some horror movie played a continual loop in her head. She swallowed hard and felt sick. "Twice."

A twitch at the corner of his mouth might have passed for a smile.

She placed a hand on her chest and drew in a deep breath. "Do you think that's funny?"

"Of course not. You smashed a wiseguy's hand in the door. If I were you, I'd think about relocating."

"For how long?"

He glanced at her, then back at the road. "Indefinitely."

"What? Like in the witness protection program?" Oh God!

He shook his head. "The government isn't prosecuting the Gallo boys or Ricky and you didn't witness anything." He glanced at her again, then back at the road. "Except smashing Lefty's hand. You witnessed that."

If she wasn't careful, she was going to freak out. "Maybe the Gallos will forget about it in a few weeks."

"Doubtful." He shook his head.

Would it kill him to lie? "You knocked Ricky out! That's worse."

"They don't know who I am."

She got the feeling he wouldn't be all that afraid if they did know. She placed a hand on her chest and drew in a shaky breath. Things just kept getting worse. "Oh God. I slammed a gangster's hand in my door."

"Twice."

Like she needed the reminder. What if Lefty Lou never got over it? Never forgot? What if he found her? She slid her hand up to her throat. No one would know to look for her. For several months no one would think to file a missing person's report. By then, she would not only be swimming with the fishes, she'd be chum. To make matters worse, it also occurred to her that she'd jumped into the SUV of a stranger. "Lefty's hand is probably only bruised." She wasn't sure, but she thought she saw stars in her peripheral vision.

"Probably broke," provided Mr. Helpful.

"Oh my God!"

"Are you going to pass out?"

"Maybe." She swallowed hard. "Probably." He looked like he was gearing up for more of his special brand of compassion and she held up her hand toward him. "Stop. Please. You're making things worse," she rambled as she tried not to think that she might have jumped from the frying pan into the fire. "I know we don't know each other at all, but you could *try* to offer some comfort. Be a little supportive, here."

He took a left exit toward the airport and asked, "How?"

Really? She had to think of supportive things for him to say? "Like you could try, 'Look, on the bright side, Stella.' "

"You broke a guy's already fucked-up hand. What's the bright side?"

It probably wasn't broken and she wished he'd quit saying that. "Well . . . I could have smashed his good hand."

"So?"

"So, this way he can still text."

He glanced across the car at her like *she* was the stone-cold one. "That's the bright side?"

It was the best she could do while trying not to freak out. To not pass out or worse, cry. She hated to cry in public. Much better to pass out. In the middle of her personal trauma, she suddenly became aware of her surroundings. They were on the expressway to Miami International Airport, and she looked out her side window at the signs. "Are you picking someone up from MIA?"

"Dropping you off."

Her head snapped toward him, and her ponytail whipped across her bare shoulder and her sunglasses slid down her nose. "Am I going somewhere?"

"Texas. I e-mailed your itinerary to your cell phone."

She looked at him over the top of her glasses. "Texas?" No one ever asked her if she wanted to go to Texas. She didn't. Anxiety pounded in her chest even as her head felt light.

"Is there somewhere else you'd rather stay for a while?"

Where she'd rather stay was impossible. Not after last night. Or early this morning, rather. Not after G.I. Joe had knocked out Ricky and she'd made everything worse by smashing Lou's hand. Not that she'd had a choice about that. He tried to break her lock, but she hadn't enjoyed hurting him. Not like the man across the car. Beau Junger clearly loved kicking ass, taking names, and sniffing "flashbang." Around the *boom-boom-boom* pounding in her head, she thought about her mom. She could go to her mother's in New Mexico. She'd be safe from the Gallos and Ricky there. But her mother hadn't always looked out for Stella. Hadn't put her before Carlos, and Stella wasn't ready to pretend everything was wonderful. To act like bad stuff had never happened, which was her mother's way of coping. If no one talked in any real way about the past, then it could be rewritten.

"I assume you have a photo ID on you."

She pushed the black frames up the bridge of her nose. "Yeah." She always carried a Visa and her driver's license in her backpack.

"You fly into Dallas, then on to Amarillo."

To stay with Sadie. She certainly wasn't ready for that. She shook her head. "This is kind of sudden."

"Did you want to stay and hang out with Lefty?"

"No." But she wasn't ready to see her sister. Especially not now. Now that her life was a steaming pile of crap. She moaned and put her fingers to her temples above the frames of her glasses. Had she moaned out loud or just in her head?

The Escalade rolled past vehicles and cabs parked along the curb of the north terminal and pulled to a stop behind a Lincoln Town Car. "Your flight leaves in an hour," she heard the voice from across the Escalade say above the noise in her head. "American Airlines, flight four-eighty-four, concourse D. You're flying first class and should have plenty of time to get through security."

"First class," she heard her own voice squeak stupidly.

"Thank your sister." He got out of the vehicle and walked around the front of the Cadillac. He moved from a slice of bright Miami sun shining in his short blond hair and on the lenses of his sunglasses, and into the shade of the metal awning. He opened the passenger door and she unbelted her seat belt with a soft click. "Sadie knows about Ricky and the Gallos?"

"No. She just knows to expect you."

Apparently, whether she wanted to be expected or not. She climbed out of the Escalade and threaded one arm through a strap of her back-pack. Once upon a time, when she'd had various reunion fantasies of Sadie, Stella had always been a success at something. Whether it had been a princess at five, a unicorn trainer at ten, or a rock star at fifteen.

"My brother, Blake, will pick you up at the airport."

A car honked somewhere and the noise and belch of shuttle bus exhaust filled the air. "How will I know who he is?" In none of her sister-reunion fantasies had she been a bartender.

"You'll know."

A bartender on the run from mobsters. "How?"

"He's my twin brother."

"There are two of you?" Even through the tangle of emotion and collision of racing thoughts in her head, she winced at the horror.

"Yeah. Twice the fun." He handed her the duffel from the rear seat. "You don't even have to check a bag."

"Oh." She didn't want to go. She really didn't, but no one cared.

He pushed her sunglasses to the top of her head and placed a big hand beneath her chin. He lifted her gaze, and his touch was warm against her skin, firm, and strangely comforting. Like a strong tether in a life that was spinning out of control. Only he was responsible for most of the spinning. Horns honked around them. Wheels on luggage clattered across the pavement as he stared at her from behind his mirrored sunglasses. She caught her reflection and inwardly flinched. She looked terrible. Pale and tired and about ready to jump out of her own skin.

"Are you going to be okay?"

She turned her face away and took a step back. What did it matter? He didn't care. Clearly he wanted to dump her at the curb and get on with his life. She pushed her glasses down and the corners of her lips up. "I'm good."

"Are you sure?" He tilted his head to one side and added with his own special brand of sensitivity, "You don't look too good."

"Thank you."

"Are you nervous about meeting your sister?"

Nervous? "No." Terrified.

"Good. She obviously wants to meet you."

She didn't know which terrified her more. The prospect of staying in Miami and running into Lefty or flying to Texas and meeting Sadie. "Wonderful." She lifted her free hand and gave a little wave. "Thanks for the ride and for rescuing me from the Gallos." Although the reason they'd been at her apartment in the first place had totally been his fault.

"Sure." He moved to the front of the SUV. "You have my card. Give my cell a call if you need anything."

She took another step back and dropped her hand. He didn't mean it. His job was done. He didn't care, and why should he? He didn't know her and didn't owe her anything. He'd been hired by Sadie to give her a message. That was it. "Okay. Bye." She turned on the worn heels of her Doc Martens and walked toward the automatic doors. They opened and she moved inside. Rows of ticket lines snaked around the roped areas, crammed with travelers. Families with small children pushed strollers and luggage. He'd said she had a first-class ticket on American Airlines. She glanced over her shoulder one last time as the SUV pulled away from the curb. Was she going to do this? Could she do this? Just get on a plane and meet her sister for the first time? People rushed past, voices pressed in on her, and her phone rang. She set her duffel on the floor, then reached inside a side pocket of her backpack and pulled it out. The number of Ricky's Rock 'N' Roll flashed across the screen. Ricky. Her scalp got tight and tingly at the thought. Or it could be Malika. Her friend and coworker had never been responsible with her cell bill and often had her phone turned off. She should tell Malika good-bye. Reassure Malika that she was okay. She stared at the phone for several more seconds, then pushed answer.

"Hello."

"Where are you?"

It wasn't Malika and she fought the urge to duck and cover at the sound of her former boss's voice. He was so mad, it sounded like he spoke from between gritted teeth.

"Tell me where you are, Stella." The last time she'd seen Ricky, he'd been a puddle of tangerine at her feet. "I won't hurt you."

Like hell.

"I just want your boyfriend's name." He paused. "Hello. Are you there?"

"He's not my boyfriend."

"Is he part of those Gorokhov bastards?" he gritted between his teeth. "He looked Russian."

"Joe?" He looked all-American.

"His name is Joe? Joe what?"

"I'd never met him before last night." Which was true. "He was just some guy in the parking lot." Which was mostly true.

"The lot video caught you leaving with him."

She'd forgotten about the security cameras in the parking lot. "Then you can probably see that I was as surprised to see him as you were." For one optimistic moment she thought she could reason with her former boss. Maybe make everything okay again. "I swear that—"

"Cut the shit!" Ricky screamed into the phone, crushing her unrealistic hope and raising the tiny hairs on the back of her neck. "Those Gorokhov bastards are cutting into my business. No one takes money out of my pocket and gets away with it. No one leans on my—What's that noise?" he interrupted himself. "Are you at the airport?"

She hit end on her phone and looked around as if she half expected Ricky or one of the Gallos to grab her. Her breath caught in her chest as she bent down and grabbed her duffel. She moved toward the first-class check-in and took her place in line. Ricky didn't know for sure she was at the airport, she told herself, but even if he acted on his suspicion, it would take a good half hour to forty-five minutes to get to MIA from the bar.

The duffel weighed down her arm as she moved forward in line. He'd have to know which terminal and line, and the odds of him actually finding her were slim to impossible. The heavy airport security calmed her nerves about her crazy former boss but did nothing for the other reason her stomach was a knot of nervous tension.

Sadie.

Stella moved forward in line. For the past few years, she'd given up her dream of meeting her sister. She'd packed it away with other childhood dreams and hadn't thought of it much. Hadn't thought of family much. Especially Sadie. Now Sadie wanted to meet her, and all the old feeling of want and hope and hurt swamped her. The one thing that Stella had wanted so desperately as a child was just a plane ticket away. A few hours from happening.

The knot in her stomach tightened as she took another step forward. With each step, it got tighter and tighter until she thought she might be sick. Her chest ached and her head got light and she tried to pull air deep into her lungs. Heat flushed her neck and cheeks, and, a few feet from the front of the line, she ducked under the rope before she fell on her face. She wove through travelers and luggage. She couldn't breathe and bumped into a businessman on a cell phone. She practically ran through the automatic doors and gasped once she was outside. She sucked humid fumes into her lungs as deep as possible.

Panic attack. She recognized it flushing her face and pounding in her head and chest. She'd had them before, only now she knew she wasn't going to die. That her heart would not explode, and if she focused on something else, she would not pass out.

All around her, people brushed past and horns honked and she walked. She didn't know where she was going. Just somewhere before the last twelve hours caught up with her and she passed out or worse. A Hilton shuttle pulled between a minivan and a cab at the curb and she kept walking. As she moved from the north to the central terminal, the sun hit her face. She paused to pull her glasses from the top of her head and shoved them on the bridge of her nose. An afternoon breeze stirred palm trees across the street of the upper-deck garden. Flags from around the world stood like sentinels at one end and fluttered in the slight wind. She moved across the road toward the oasis in the midst of concrete and steel and glass. The weight of her duffel pulled at her arm as she dodged a black truck and almost got mowed down by a Prius. She found a bench hidden within the greenery and sank onto it.

The duffel and backpack dropped at her feet and she raised her face. She took deep, shaky, breaths and shut her eyes. Her heart wasn't going to explode, she told herself. She wasn't going to die. She wasn't going to pass out if she slowed her breathing and calmed down.

For some reason, the thought of getting on a plane and living out her childhood dream had finally shoved her into the panic attack she'd been avoiding since Ricky had grabbed her last night. It scared her more than mobsters busting into her apartment. Although that had scared her plenty.

She slowly let her breath out and placed her forearms on her thighs. Sadie had hired Beau Junger to find her. Sadie wanted to meet Stella. So what was so scary? What had kept her from getting on that American flight to Texas?

Stella relaxed her shoulders and stared at the toes of her boots. What was she afraid of? she asked herself, even though she knew the answer. Long ago she'd figured out that sometimes people just didn't like her. Whether it was her sense of humor or her outlook on life, some people didn't think she was as funny as she thought she was. Others didn't like her lack of focus. She did seem to flit from job to job and place to place. There were even those in her own family who didn't like her. They called her *guera*. White girl, and they didn't mean it in a good way. They thought she was spoiled because of her father's money, but the money had never been hers. The trust was in her name, but she'd never had any control over it.

Tears stung the backs of Stella's eyes. She felt like a kid again, lying on her bed, alone in her room as one of her biggest fears rolled through her head. *What if Sadie didn't like her?* She'd rather live her whole life not knowing her sister than have Sadie look at her like some people did. Like their own father had.

As the first tear dripped on the lens of her big sunglasses, the toes of black tactical boots appeared before her blurred vision.

"You're going to miss your flight."

She was almost relieved to hear his deep familiar voice. "How'd you find me?"

"Your cell has a GPS."

She looked up. Up past his long legs and flat stomach, over his big chest and thick neck to the frown pulling at his mouth. "You got here pretty fast."

"I hadn't gone far."

Her gaze continued to his gray eyes drilling into her. "Is Sadie paying you to make sure I get on the plane?"

"No. I pulled into short-term to make some business calls."

With the sun pouring over his broad shoulders, he looked bigger than ever. "And to make sure I got on the plane."

A sharp nod confirmed her suspicion. "The next one doesn't take off for three hours."

"Yeah." She took off her sunglasses and wiped a tear from her cheek with the back of her hand. "I can't get on it."

"Why?"

She shrugged. "I just . . ." She lifted the hem of her dress and cleaned the lens of her glasses. "I don't like heights."

"You're afraid to fly?"

She nodded. Much better to lie than tell him that she was afraid her sister wouldn't like her.

"Why didn't you say that? I would have made other arrangements."

"You didn't ask." She returned the glasses to her face. "You just shoved a ticket at me."

He pulled out his phone and punched a few numbers. "Yeah," he spoke into his cell. "I need you to look at bus schedules in Miami and find a ticket headed to Amarillo."

Stella stood. She didn't know what she was going to do, but it for damn sure didn't involve a bus. "Forget it. I'm not getting on a freaking bus."

His scowl reached his eyes. "I'll have to get back to you." He ended his conversation and shoved the phone in his pocket. "What are your plans, Stella?"

Wow. That was frosty. Good. She liked frosty. It kind of snapped her out of her fog. She reached for her backpack and put it over one shoulder. "I don't know. Maybe I'll . . ." What? "Maybe I'll rent a car and go . . ." She stooped to pick up her duffel. "Somewhere for a while." Until Ricky forgot about her. It couldn't take too long. Could it?

Mr. Stone Cold stared down at her. "Un-fucking-believable," he said. "This was supposed to be easy. Just give you a fucking message and get the fuck out of town."

Wow, not only was he stone cold, he apparently liked the F-bombs. "Sorry." She shrugged. "But you can leave now. You gave me the message from Sadie. I'll be okay." And she would. She'd been taking care of herself for the past ten years. Most of her life, really. She'd figure out something. She didn't need help. Not from anyone. Especially from a man who was so cold he probably crapped ice cubes.

Chapter Four

He was hot. The kind of hot that had nothing to do with the ninety-degree temperature outside. Beau Junger directed the air vents toward his face and glanced across the rented Escalade at the twenty-eight-year-old sacked out on his leather seat. A white iPad sat on her lap and a pair of purple ear buds plugged her head with music. As far as Beau had been able to surmise from her annoying singing before she'd fallen asleep, she listened to indie crap.

Right before she'd crashed, she'd taken the rubber band from her ponytail and pulled her hair over one shoulder. The long black strands lay on her tan skin and curled beneath the curve of her breast. Shiny like the night before.

Damn. Beau pulled his gaze from her hair and smooth skin and turned his attention to the interstate heading toward Naples and Tampa. She was twenty-eight. Even if he wasn't determined to keep it in his pants and wait until sex meant something, she was too young. Much too young for him to have thoughts of his fingers tangled in her hair.

He scowled and moved his head from side to side to get the kinks out. How had this happened? How had things gone bat-shit sideways so fast? He'd agreed to do Vince a simple favor. Vince was a good guy. A friend of Blake's. Beau was just supposed to give Stella the message that her sister wanted to contact her. Easy. Nothing to it, and he'd had business in Miami and Tampa anyway. He'd provided security a few nights before at the wedding of a rock star in Key Biscayne. Except for the helos buzzing overhead, drunken guests, and partiers having sex in the bushes, the event had been blessedly uneventful. No breach in security or punches thrown.

He couldn't say the same for the favor he'd agreed to do for Vince. He'd known within minutes of arriving at Ricky's Rock 'N' Roll that he was walking into a goat screw. His first clue had been the drag queen in tight leather cracking a whip on stage. He should have turned around and walked out, but he'd never been a guy to give up. To call it quits. Not even when the queen with the green lips had called him Joe and wanted to see his "weapon." But being propositioned by a queen hadn't annoyed him as much as the men groping each other around him. He'd bugged out to escape all the writhing and dry humping. He'd grabbed a bite to eat at a Cuban café and then he'd waited it out in the parking lot behind the bar. Hanging out in the lot, making calls and catching up on business, had been preferable to hanging with queens and horny gay men.

He could understand a guy being born gay. He wasn't into other men, but understood the biology of it. What he didn't understand was why a guy would put on a dress and heels and purposely tape his junk to his ass. Nor did he understand dry humping in public. Gay or straight, he'd never been into public displays of affection. He wasn't a prude, far from it. He just didn't understand why anyone would get himself all worked up in public. Get busy at a party or on a dance floor when there was probably a perfectly good bedroom or hotel or closet nearby.

Beau adjusted the vent beneath the steering column and glanced at his passenger out of the corners of his eyes before returning his gaze to the road. Her face was turned away from his, her head resting back against the seat. She was blessedly quiet for once. She was asleep, but she'd had to wonder what the hell she was going to do with herself now. Now that she'd been fired, pissed off a couple of mobsters, and couldn't go home. He was wondering the same thing. What in the hell was he going to do with Estella Immaculata Leon-Hollowell? It wasn't like she was his responsibility. He'd done the favor for Vince. He'd given her the message. His job was finished.

Why did he feel responsible?

Maybe because he'd played a part in her present situation. He was in security and knew how to talk to unpredictable people. To handle drunks and deescalate volatile situations without the use of physical force, but he'd wanted to hit Ricky De Luca. The second the man had grabbed her and refused to let her go, he'd wanted to knock him out. Hell, he thought he'd been fairly reasonable, giving the guy three seconds and two chances, but Ricky had told him to fuck off. Twice, and that had been one time too many.

Beau passed a semi loaded with produce, then moved back into the right lane. But if he hadn't clocked Ricky, the man wouldn't have sicced the Gallo boys on Stella and Beau wouldn't feel responsible for her now.

He could have left her at the airport. She'd even told him to leave and that she'd be okay.

So why hadn't he?

Maybe because in the light of day, sitting on a bench with her backpack and duffel, she'd looked so young. So much younger and more innocent than her full red lips and leopard bustier had implied the night before. To say nothing of her little leather shorts. Jesus, her ass had been amazing and—He stopped his mental wandering. He didn't want to think of her little butt in those little shorts. Or her red lips and what she could do to him. Not even the old Beau would have gone there. The old Beau who woke up in strange beds with nameless women. Even that Beau had a few standards. Admittedly very few, but one unbreakable rule was never have sex with a client. Another was never knock boots with a buddy's sister. He'd learned that one the hard way, and Stella Leon was both. A client and Vince's future sister-in-law. *And* she was too young.

He glanced at the navigation system in the center of the dashboard. He'd been celibate for eight months. Eight months since he'd picked up a cocktail waitress in a Chicago bar. Eight months since he'd looked in a hotel mirror and saw his father looking back at him.

He'd spent a lot of his life proving he was nothing like Captain William T. Junger. His old man was a legend in the SEAL teams. A hard-as-nails warrior who'd earned his reputation in Vietnam and Grenada and countless other clandestine engagements. He was a hero. A leader. Loyal to the teams and his country. If you read a book about the history of Navy SEALs, several paragraphs were always dedicated to Captain Junger's contribution to the teams. A lot of words dedicated to his courage and valor. Words like "tough," "brave," "honorable" were used to describe him. He was all of those things, but what no one ever wrote about, what no one mentioned, was that he was also a ruthless philanderer.

On the surface, the Jungers had looked like the perfect military family. Handsome Navy captain, beautiful blond wife, and two healthy sons. He and Blake had excelled at everything: school, sports, Boy Scouts. Beau couldn't recall anyone ever telling him or Blake that they had to be the best. They'd just always known. Not only did they have their father's blood in their veins, they lived with his expectations and reputation. They went to bed with it and woke with it in the morning.

Teachers, coaches, and random adults expected them to run faster. Swim farther. Hit harder. Naturally competitive, they always gave their best. They pushed themselves and each other, and if they somehow fell short, they tried again. Beau and Blake idolized their father. He was bigger than life and they loved him as much as they feared him. The captain never punished with his hands. He didn't have to. One look from his gray eyes cut to the soul. The look he'd perfected to intimidate Uncle Sam's enemies, be they terrorists, drug lords, or thugs, intimidated the hell out of his sons. If the look wasn't punishment enough for the old man, he made the boys do push-ups until their muscles trembled and burned.

Amid all the tough, hard edges of their lives was their mother, Naomi Junger. The one person who loved them no matter the color of the ribbons they won. Naomi had been a sweet girl from North Carolina when she'd met and married William Junger. She was beautiful and vivacious, with an infectious laugh, and her warm accent and soft touch had filled the Junger home with unconditional love. As long as they remembered to say "please" and "thank you" and put their dinner napkins in their laps, the twin brothers never heard a critical word from her lips. She kept a perfect house. Cooked perfect meals. Looked perfect, even when their father was deployed or away training.

Perfect, except for the days when she didn't get out of bed. When she sobbed like she would never stop, and when pain took over her beautiful face. When she learned that her husband had once again betrayed her with another woman.

For about the first ten years of his life, Beau hadn't had a clue why his mother had days that seemed like her life had been drained from her. It wasn't until he'd heard his parents arguing about it, when he heard his mother's raised voice for the first time, that he learned of his father's infidelity. That he learned his father caused so much pain. Time and again. That day, he learned that his father wasn't a hero.

He'd talked to Blake about what he'd heard. His brother said they should try and forget about it. Their parents had fought it out and their father had to stop now. Of course he hadn't, but there hadn't been any more fighting about it. No more raised voices or yelling. Not until Beau was seventeen, but the fight hadn't been between his mother and father.

They'd been living in a white stucco house, a few miles from the base in Coronado, California. He and Blake had applied to the Naval Academy the year before and were heading for Annapolis in a few months. There was never a question about what they would do with their lives. Never any thought about their future but that they would follow in their father's footsteps. Together. From the womb to the tomb.

Never any thought until he found his mother in her big closet, lying on a pile of clothes she'd pulled from hangers.

"Why do you stay?" he asked her.

She gave a very slight lift of one shoulder, as if a full shrug would be just too much effort. "Where would I go?"

He wanted her to get up. To do something, but she just stared at the toes of his shoes. "Where is he?" he asked, as angry at her as he was at his father.

"With Joyce."

"The neighbor?" The one who wore her clothes too tight and her hair several shades too blond? The neighbor that everyone knew had a lot of "boyfriends"? His mother was ten times more attractive and had twenty times the class.

She nodded, and Beau was out of the house and pounding on the next door before he even thought of what he would do if his father answered. Those few moments he stood on that porch, the warm California sun heating his already hot face, seemed to drag on forever. He raised a hand to knock once more when the door opened and Joyce stood in the darker entrance. Her hair a tangled mess, a silky robe hanging off one shoulder, she looked her part. And as Beau stood there, staring at the neighborhood bike, a desperate part of him hoped like hell his father wasn't in this woman's house.

"Where's my father?"

She pushed the door open farther as his father walked up behind her, pulling his brown T-shirt over his head. "What do you need?" There was no shame or guilt. He looked more annoyed than anything.

"How can you do this to my mother?"

"She shouldn't have sent you over here."

"She didn't." He looked into his father's eyes. Cool gray and so much like his own. "Why do you hurt her like this?"

"A man needs more than one woman can give him. Someday you'll understand."

"What? That cheating on my wife is okay?"

"It's what men do. You'll do it, too."

No. He'd seen the devastation in his mother's eyes too many times to ever cause a person he loved that much pain. He shook his head. "No, I won't."

His father smiled as if he knew better. "You and your brother are just like me."

"I'm not like you," he'd protested, and then he'd set out to prove it. The next day he'd walked into a recruiter's office and enlisted in the Marines.

An enlisted man.

The Marines.

The old man had been *pissed*. His mother worried that he'd made a rash decision out of anger. His brother had been in shock, but Beau had never regretted it. Out from beneath the shadow of his father, he'd thrived in the corps. He'd been his own man. Discovered a freedom from his last name. An independence from impossible expectations that his brother would never know in the teams. No matter that Blake was twice the SEAL that their father had ever been.

Until that morning eight months ago, he'd

thought that he was nothing like the old man. Yeah, he loved a good adrenaline rush. He loved clandestine missions and a well-placed bullet. And yeah, he'd had sex with a lot of different women all over the world. He'd had a few relationships along the way, but he'd never been married. Didn't have a family to devastate. Didn't have to look in the face of a wife and kids and see their disgust because once again he'd had meaningless sex with a meaningless woman.

He'd only had his own face to look at, and he'd never felt disgust at the man looking back at him. Not until that morning eight months ago. Maybe it was age. Maybe it was settling into civilian life. Maybe it was his mother harping about family. Whatever it was, he wanted more. More than meaningless sex with meaningless women.

He knew a lot of men didn't understand why that meant celibacy. His brother didn't understand. Hell, Beau didn't think he understood completely, but he didn't believe in half measures. When he committed to something, he went all the way. The next time he had sex, it would be with the woman he wanted to spend the rest of his life loving. A woman who was mature. Calm. Secure in her own skin. Stable. Not overly romantic, because he wasn't a romantic guy. At his age, he expected she'd have a couple of kids. He liked kids. He expected to add a few more.

A woman who liked sex so he wouldn't have to

go without sex ever again. He'd read that the longer a person went without, the easier it got. He didn't find that to be the case. Perhaps he didn't think about sex as much as he used to, but when he did, the urges were as strong. He'd just learned a few tricks to take his mind off his urges. To rewrite the script. He avoided being alone with females, and if that was impossible, he stopped any sexual thoughts he might have. Whether they were the actual thoughts of intercourse or just wondering about a tight butt in a pair of leather booty shorts.

He glanced at the girl in the next seat. Sunlight poured through the tinted windows and shone in her coal-black hair spilling down one arm. A soft flow of air from the vents in the dash picked up several strands and brushed them across her throat. One hand loosely held her iPad. The other rested in her lap, her palm up, open. The soft air that picked up strands of her hair teased the hem of her blue dress across her tan thighs.

What kind of woman jumped in a car with a virtual stranger and fell asleep? Beau returned his gaze to the highway stretching in front of him like a gray ribbon. Either she was too trusting, she didn't have other options, or she was crazy. Maybe she was all three.

Whatever her motive, he'd been damn relieved to see her practically flying down those concrete stairs with her backpack and duffel. He'd made the plan simple and easy to follow, but civilians were unpredictable, and the last thing he'd wanted to do was waste time running up those stairs and pounding on a locked door. The last thing he'd wanted to do was duke it out with the Gallos because Estella Leon couldn't follow simple directions.

He lifted a hand from the steering wheel and looked at his wristwatch. It was a little after three and he was exhausted. He'd had little sleep in the past few days and he was running on fumes.

There had been a time in his life when he'd been able to exist for days on little shut-eye. When he'd stalked the enemy and hid in shadows and on rooftops or high in the Hindu Kush. But those days were behind him. He was thirty-eight. He'd been out of the corps for several years. Long enough to get used to the luxury of more than three hours here and there.

Above the sound of the air-conditioning, a drowsy sigh and a soft *mmm* brushed across his skin and drew his attention to the next seat. Drowsy eyes the color of a Bora Bora lagoon looked back at him from Stella's beautiful face. "I fell asleep." Sleepy confusion dragged her voice to a sultry whisper. The kind of sultry voice he hadn't heard in eight months.

"About an hour ago."

She stretched her bare legs, then stared out the windshield. "Where are we?"

Eight long months since he'd slid his hands up bare legs and put his mouth on a soft throat. "South of Tampa."

"Where are we going?"

Eight months since his mouth slid south and— Jesus. That was twice. Twice since she'd jumped into his vehicle. He scowled and cleared his throat. "Tampa."

"Why Tampa?"

"My mother and Dr. Mike live in Tampa."

Two years after he and Blake had left home, his mother had shocked everyone when she finally picked herself up and walked out on his father. A year shy of her fortieth birthday, Naomi had gone back to school and earned her nursing diploma. She'd moved to Tampa, met prominent cardiologist Dr. Mike Crandall, and they'd been married for the last ten years. Happily, as far as Beau could tell.

"Are you planning to dump me on your mom?"

He glanced at her, then back at the road. He hadn't thought of that, but the idea had merit. It would certainly solve his problem of where to stash her until he figured out what to do with her. She wasn't his concern anyway. She was more Blake's responsibility than his. If he decided to "dump" her at his mother's for a few days, it wasn't like he'd be dumping her at a Travelodge.

Chapter Five

It was a mansion. With an elevator in the garage and a pair of matching Mercedes beside a row of vintage cars.

"I'm starving," Beau said as they stepped from the elevator. His arm brushed hers, warm skin and hard muscles. For some strange reason, this stranger's touch calmed the tumble in her stomach. A steady touch in this strange, unsteady world that she'd woken to this morning. The heels of their boots thudded in perfect time as they walked down a short hall to an enormous kitchen. "You hungry?"

She'd had a bagel that morning and her stomach had started growling an hour ago. She nodded, speechless for one of the few times in her life. Everything was white. Shiny white marble like a museum. Stella had seen houses like this only in magazines or on television. She'd never been in a gated community in her life and felt very much out of place. She was careful not to scuff up the marble floor with the black soles of her boots.

"My mother knows our ETA." Beau's deep voice seemed to kind of echo, or maybe it was her nerves ricocheting in her own head. "She'll have something for us."

Stella walked beside Beau from the rear of the

house toward the front. A lot of her family worked for people who lived in houses like this. Stella's mother and grandmother didn't, but they certainly had at one time. Before Stella was born. Before Marisol had given birth to a rich man's illegitimate child and been paid to stay away. "She knows *I'm* with you?"

"Of course."

Of course. That was it. No reassuring, "She's fine with it, Stella. Relax." Years ago Stella had come to the realization that she was an acquired taste. More like schnapps than cognac. Which was fine with her. Schnapps was more fun than stuffy old cognac, but this was one of those times in her life when it might be best to be cognac.

She glanced through the rooms at the white furniture, deep purple and red pillows, and silver tables. Huge windows looked out on the back terrace and the Gulf of Mexico beyond. "Did you grow up here?" In the entrance, a wide white marble staircase and black wrought-iron rails led to a second floor. Paintings and professional photographs were artistically hung on the walls, and a vase of fresh-cut flowers dominated the heavy table in the center. Stella looked up at the domed ceiling high above her head.

"No. Dr. Mike is Mother's second husband," said the man of few words. Giving nothing more than the barest information.

A spot of yellow caught Stella's eye and she

turned her attention to the woman at the top of the stairs. Even from a distance Stella could see that she was perfect. Perfect blond hair, perfect lemon-colored blouse and white pants. Perfect woman in a perfect house, and Stella became very aware of her nonperfect appearance. Of her wrinkled dress and scuffed boots. She'd found an elastic band in the bottom of her backpack and had pulled her hair into a ponytail. The closer the perfect woman moved toward them, the more Stella felt imperfect, and the more she felt an urge to hide behind the stone mountain of a man standing beside her. Just slide behind him and hide her face in the warmth of his back. Although she didn't know why she thought she'd find comfort there or why she was being such a weenie. Usually she was much stronger. She'd learned to be strong at a young age, and instead of hiding, she squared her shoulders and stood a little taller. Well, as tall as possible given her height.

"Beau!" A blond bob brushed the other woman's shoulders and a twisted strand of pearls circled her throat. She was tall and thin and beautiful, and the tiny heels of her shoes tapped across the floor as she moved toward her son.

"Mom." Beau dropped Stella's duffel at his feet and opened his arms as his mother disappeared inside. He dipped his head and spoke next to her ear. His mother nodded and pulled back.

"Love you, too." She gazed up and put her hands

on the sides of his square jaw and cupped his face. "You look tired, baby boy."

Baby boy? Stella bit the corner of her lip. He looked like neither a baby nor a boy.

"Getting old."

"No, you're not." Her hands fell to his big shoulders. "If you're getting old, that means I'm getting really old."

"You'll never look old, Ma." He cracked a rare smile and glanced up at the second floor. "Is Dr. Mike around?"

"No." She shook her head and took a step back. "He's speaking at a cardiovascular diseases conference in Cleveland."

Beau returned his gaze to his mother, and a crease pulled at his brows. "You always travel with him. You didn't stay because of me, did you?"

"Of course. I'd rather be here with you than sitting around with a bunch of doctors talking about atrial fibrillation." Her hands fell to the sides of her crisp linen pants. "I love spending time with Mike, but after a few hours of the latest treatments and curative therapies discussions, I have to excuse myself and find something else to do." She turned and looked at Stella, her brown gaze intense and a little curious. Tension pinched between Stella's shoulders as she stood still and as tall as possible. Then a warm smile curved the older woman's lips and reached the lines at the corners of her eyes. Eyes that were a warm brown instead of cold gray like her son's. She reached out and took Stella's hand in a soft cool grasp, and Stella felt her shoulders relax. "You must be Beau's friend. I'm his mother, Naomi Crandall."

Friend? She wouldn't call him a *friend.* Although she didn't know what to call him. Uptight hard-ass, maybe. "It's nice to meet you, Mrs. Crandall."

"Naomi." She gave Stella's hand a little squeeze, then dropped her own to her side. "Goodness, you're a pretty little thing."

"Jesus," Beau muttered.

"Don't curse, son. You know I don't put up with cursing in my home."

Stella cast a glance at the grouch by her side, then back at his much more pleasant mother. "You have a lovely home, Naomi."

"Oh, it's a museum." She waved aside the compliment. "But we entertain Mike's hospital associates and host charity events here."

Stella had never been to a charity event, although she did stuff money in the Salvation Army kettles at Christmas.

"Are you hungry?" Naomi asked Stella as she took a step back.

Beau picked up Stella's duffel. "I'm starving."

"You were born starving." She turned, and they followed her through a room with Grecian-inspired columns and a massive stone fireplace. "I had a wonderful shrimp and avocado salad, crab ceviche, and chilled salmon with dill sauce prepared for you."

Sounded yummy to Stella. She loved ceviche. Crab or cucumber, it didn't matter.

"Cold fish?" Beau complained. "Anything else?"

"Of course. A beautiful flatbread and a sprouted wheat."

He grumbled something that sounded suspiciously like cursing again. "This isn't one of your do-gooder meetings, and I'm not one of your Lean Cuisine friends."

"It's heart healthy."

"My heart is healthy enough."

"Your heart can never be too healthy." She opened a set of glass doors and stepped onto a veranda overlooking a stunning view of the gulf beyond. "Just last week, a thirty-year-old man came into St. Joseph's presenting left main coronary artery stenosis."

Stella breathed in the breeze of the gulf. She didn't know anyone who lived like this. She doubted even Sadie with all her money lived like this.

"My heart is fine and I want red meat." He dropped their bags just outside the door. "Rare."

Naomi moved toward a table set with bright red serving plates and baskets of bread and pretended not to hear her son. "I read an article published in Mike's *American Heart Association Journal* that people who have type A, B, or AB blood have an increased risk of heart disease. You and your brother have type A. Like William."

"Last time I talked to Dad, he sounded healthy." Beau picked up a dinner plate and loaded it up with food.

"The ceviche is fabulous," she told Stella as Stella picked up a plate. Then she turned her attention back to her son. "Everyone sounds healthy until they are hit with the 'widow maker.' " She reached for bottle of wine chilling in a silver ice bucket. "Pinot?"

"Yes, please," Stella said as she put a spoonful of shrimp and avocado salad on her plate. Her elbow bumped Beau's forearm, and she felt him tense beside her like she'd done something wrong. Displeasure tightened the corners of his mouth. "This looks wonderful, Naomi." She took a healthy mound of ceviche and a piece of fish and decided not to even try and figure him out. She grabbed a hunk of bread, then followed Beau to a small glass-and-wrought-iron table set with cloth napkins and silver flatware. A striped umbrella shaded the table, and Stella sat in the shade across from the man who'd changed her life with one punch to Ricky's jaw. She'd known Beau less than twenty-four hours, yet here she sat, on the veranda of a multimillion-dollar mansion with him and his mother and feeling surprisingly at ease. Oh, she felt out of place, to be sure, but not nervous or panicked. Maybe it was because Naomi was calm and welcoming and seemed genuinely kind. Unlike her son, who was more like a barely contained thunderstorm. Or maybe it was because after the last twenty-four hours, she just felt numb. Like a train wreck victim who didn't feel the pain of a large, gaping wound due to traumatic shock.

Naomi set three glasses of wine on the table and pushed one toward Stella. "I'm assuming you're over twenty-one, Stella."

"Yes." She smiled and took a drink. She knew she looked young, but not *that* young. The crisp pinot hit her tongue and left behind a hint of pear. "This is wonderful," she said, meaning more than just the wine.

"I'm happy you like it."

Beau unfolded his napkin and placed it in his lap as he watched his mother take a seat. "Why aren't you eating?"

"I ate earlier."

"You're too thin."

"I ate!" Naomi insisted, and as the other two discussed Naomi's eating habits, Stella stabbed her fork into a big piece of shrimp and avocado and took a bite. She was even hungrier than she thought and had to remember to slow down and not scarf like a wild beast. She placed her napkin in her lap and had to remind herself to use her best table manners, too.

Stella loved good wine and good food. She

rarely cooked for just herself, but growing up, she'd certainly done her share. Besides family meals, twice a year she and her mother and Abuela made tamales for the entire family. It took them from sunup to sundown, and the tamales were devoured within hours. Sometimes when she let herself, she missed standing beside her mother and grandmother within the steamy kitchen in Las Cruces. She missed her mother's busy hands and the sound of Abuela's rich voice competing with *Una Familia con Suerte* blaring from the television on the kitchen counter. Most of the time, though, she didn't let herself miss them at all. Most of the time, she pushed those feelings and memories to the back of her mind where they couldn't hurt her.

"Mmm."

"You okay?"

She didn't realize she'd closed her eyes until she opened them and looked across the table into Beau's narrowed gray gaze. A shadow from the umbrella slashed across his forehead and nose and the chiseled bones of his cheek and jaw. She wondered what she'd done now. Not that she cared that much. "I'm fine. Why?"

"You moaned." He stabbed at his salmon like the fish had committed a felony.

"Really?" He was mad because she *moaned?* That was ridiculous, and she turned her attention to his mother. "I moaned?"

"I wouldn't call that a moan." Naomi took a sip of wine. "More like a little sound of pleasure."

"Call it what you want." Beau shrugged. "Sound of pleasure. Breathy moan. It's the same sound."

Her moan had been breathy? He made it sound sexual and she hadn't even been thinking of sex. Not at all.

"Don't embarrass our guest." An amused little smile tipped Naomi's lips. "Beau's never brought a woman to meet me before."

After everything she'd been through in the past twenty-four hours, sex was the last thing on her mind. Until now. Until he'd put it out there on the table like a dessert course. Stella looked at the man scowling at his mother as he chewed. His Adam's apple moved up his thick neck when he swallowed. She couldn't imagine getting naked with Beau. He just wasn't her type. She liked skinny guys with a sensitive side who weren't afraid to show it. She liked guys who wrote poems and song lyrics, and she didn't even mind a little nail polish or eyeliner every now and then. She couldn't imagine that Beau *had* a sensitive side. Let alone that he wrote poems or wore eyeliner. The thought of him painting his nails made her smile.

"Don't start picking out wedding china and counting grandkids, Ma." He reached for his wineglass, and the evening sun caught on the rim and in short strands of his blond hair. He was handsome, though. If a girl liked big guys with hard muscles and chiseled good looks. "I told you on the phone, I'm doing a favor for one of Blake's buddies." He took a drink, then set the glass next to his plate. "I'm just making sure Stella gets to her sister's place in Texas."

That was news to Stella and she forgot all about picturing him with black fingernails. "You are?"

"We'll talk later," he said, and dug into his dinner.

She flipped her hair over one shoulder and returned his scowl. "I'm not taking the bus."

Naomi gasped. "Beau, you are not dumping this girl at the Greyhound station!"

"You're right, I'm not," he said without taking his attention from Stella. "I think we covered that at the airport. You're afraid to fly and hate the bus. Those two options are off the table."

Stella took a sip of wine and asked the million-dollar question. "What's on the table?"

"I'm working on it." He took a big bite of salmon and washed it down with pinot. "What about your family?"

"What about them?"

"Any of them able to drive you to Texas?"

"My mother can't leave my grandmother." She took a few bites of ceviche and swallowed. She hadn't spoken to some of her uncles in about ten years. She didn't see any reason to reconnect now. "There's no other family."

He stared at her with cool gray eyes that knew better. "Friends?"

She could probably shake loose a friend or two who might want to get out of town for a few. The Texas panhandle wasn't exactly a vacation destination, but it wasn't an armpit. Of course, she'd never been in the panhandle and couldn't say for sure. "No." She looked into her glass and swirled her wine. But she *did* know one thing for sure, she'd never said she wanted to go to Lovett, Texas. Never said she wanted a long-lost sister reunion.

"Where in Texas are you planning to visit?" Naomi asked.

It was a normal question. One that anyone would naturally ask. "My father's cattle ranch just outside of Lovett." She looked up and frowned at the man half covered in shadow and eating his salmon and ceviche like it was his favorite meal. As if he hadn't just been complaining about it. "At least I assume that's where Sadie is living in Texas."

He nodded his head as he ate but he didn't look up.

For the first eighteen years of her life, men had tried to control her, never really caring what she wanted or how she felt. "What if I say no?"

He lifted his gaze, and his gray eyes locked with hers as he chewed. "Do you want to go back to your apartment?"

That wasn't an option and he knew it.

"I'm sure Beau would never force you to go somewhere you didn't want to go. Isn't that right?"

"Right," he answered, but he didn't bother to sound very convincing. He looked down at his plate and stabbed an avocado.

Naomi raised a slim hand, and her fingers played with the collar of her yellow blouse. "I've never heard of Lovett."

"It's a little town in the panhandle about fifty miles north of Amarillo." Stella took a big bite of shrimp salad and washed it down with a bigger swallow of wine.

"I was born and raised in a town no bigger than a speck on a map. Growing up, I hated it." Naomi rose and returned with the bottle of wine. "Now looking back, some of my fondest memories are of Mama and Daddy dancing at the Grange and us kids packed up tight in the back of Daddy's truck." She poured out and added, "I love everything big cities have to offer, but small towns are a great place to grow up. Don't you think?"

Naomi assumed Stella had lived in Lovett. That was a normal assumption, she supposed. "I was born and raised in Las Cruces, New Mexico. I've never been near Lovett." She picked up her glass. She'd eaten very little that day and could feel the beginning of a nice warm glow. "Thank you."

"You're welcome." Naomi set the bottle on the

table and looked from Stella to Beau, then back again. "Never?"

Stella didn't usually talk about her personal life with people she didn't know. Some of it was embarrassing, but no doubt Beau had plugged her name into some super-secret spy software that he'd bought along with his flashbang, and he already knew everything about her. The good, the bad, and the ugly. He'd probably seen her third grade report card and the balance on her Victoria's Secret credit card. Beau would know if she was omitting, fudging, or outright lying. "Well, technically, I suppose I have been on the ranch," she said as Naomi took her seat. "I was conceived there." She reached for her glass and smiled. "Obviously, I was too young to remember the event. Thank God." No one laughed at her little joke, but she thought she was pretty dang funny. She took a drink and looked over the rim into Naomi's calm gaze. Curiosity lined her brow as she patiently waited for Stella to continue. "Sadie's mama died when she was five, and my mother was her nanny." Stella set the glass back on the table and decided just to share the short version. "To make a short story even shorter, my mother grew up really poor," she said, repeating what she'd heard too many times to count. "From the time she was able, she worked at the Super 8 and El Sombrero. The only way out of her family's house was to marry one of the neighborhood boys and have five children in as many years." She gathered her hair at the back of her neck and pulled it over one shoulder. "She wanted something different and answered an ad placed by a nanny agency. Her first placement was on the JH Ranch, in the Texas panhandle." She thought of the old photograph of her mother that Abuela had taken the day she'd left for Texas. In the faded photo she'd looked so young and pretty, and excitement sparkled in her eyes. "She worked at the ranch for three months when she discovered she was pregnant." She still couldn't picture her young mother and grouchy Clive Hollowell knocking boots. "When she told my father, he sent her back to New Mexico and paid her to stay there."

Naomi sucked in a breath. "Your mother must have been devastated."

"As my grandmother says, *Fue por lana y salio trasquilado*. She went looking for wool and came back shorn." Good Lord. The wine was doing more than casting a warm glow if she was really quoting her grandmother. Abuela had a million sayings and wasn't afraid to use them. A million annoying myths and legends and rules that she wasn't afraid to share.

"Sometimes I don't understand men." Naomi was clearly appalled. "How could a father do something like that?"

Stella didn't know which was worse. That her

father had slept with the help, or that her mother had slept with her boss. That her father had slept with a girl thirty-five years younger than he, or that her mother had taken one look at Senor Hollowell and had seen a big house and lots of money. "I didn't really know him. I only saw him about five times in my life." While her mother had gone looking for wool, she hadn't exactly been shorn. She didn't get the big house, but she got a nicer house in a nicer Las Cruces neighborhood. She didn't get Clive Hollowell's millions, but she got enough money to support her and her family. Stella wouldn't say her mother got pregnant on purpose, but she wouldn't call it an accident, either.

"Is that it?" Naomi asked.

The last time she'd seen her father, she'd been eleven. She'd wanted desperately for him to like her, but he hadn't. "He brought me porcelain horses once. I played with them until their legs broke off." That sounded so pathetic that she might have blushed if not for the pinot. She wasn't that little girl anymore who desperately wanted her father and sister to love her. She hadn't been that girl for a long time.

"That's sad."

She shook her head. "No. I . . . ah . . . liked horses more than dolls." Which was true. She glanced across the table at Beau, who seemed more interested in his plate than in her. Good.

"My father might not have wanted to know me, but he made sure my mother had money to support me. I turned out okay. I wasn't a bad kid."

Beau looked up. His face was impassive but his gray eyes stared into her as if he could see into her brain and knew all her secrets. He'd said he knew her work history. Or had that been her arrest record?

"Well, except for the time I got in trouble for spray painting unicorns on the I–25 overpass," she babbled before she could stop herself.

He raised a brow.

"It was funny," she defended herself. "And a lot cuter than skulls and stupid gang symbols." Too bad the police had not seen the humor of a cute little fantasy creature among the hardcore symbols. She'd been fourteen and had been given ten hours of community service. "On paper, my juvenile record might look like I was a trouble-maker, but it was tame stuff compared to other kids." She thought a moment, then confessed because she was sure Beau knew anyway, "Well, okay, except for shoplifting that padded bra from Kmart. That was bad. Real bad, but all the other girls in the seventh grade had boobs and I didn't. The boys used to call me names like sunken chest." She glanced at Naomi, who would surely understand. The other woman had her glass poised in front of her mouth, her eyes wide. "I just wanted to fit in and my mom wouldn't give me money for a padded bra. But that's the worst thing I ever did." She returned her gaze to Beau. "Right?"

One of his brows rose up his tan forehead. "How would I know?"

She lifted a hand, then let it fall to the table. "Because you're a spy." Duh.

Naomi laughed. "Beau, did you tell Stella you're CIA?"

"Of course not." A familiar scowl creased the corners of his eyes. "We talked about this already. I told you that I'm not a spy."

That was true. He'd said that, but he acted like one.

"He's a Marine."

A Marine. Of course he was. It all fit. The thick neck. The short hair. The hard ass. The—Wait! She'd just confessed to stealing a padded bra to a Marine. This time the pinot didn't stop the blush creeping up her neck and warming her cheeks. Stella tipped up her glass and drained it.

"Beau joined the Marines." Pride shone in Naomi's brown eyes. "He's a HOG."

Stella choked a little in the back of her throat. He certainly ate a lot, but his table manners looked acceptable to her. Last night he'd kind of gobbled down his flan, but she wouldn't call him a hog.

"My other son, Blake, followed their father into the Navy, but when the boys were little they used to play Batman and Robin."

Beau removed his gaze from Stella's and turned his attention to his mother. "We used to *fight* over who was Batman and who was Robin."

"Yes." Naomi sighed as if those were the days. "It got so bad, I had to buy one of you a Batman costume and the other Superman. They were just precious."

"Then we fought over who was more hardcore. Batman or Superman."

"The two of you still do." Naomi frowned, and suddenly looked a lot like her son. "Just last Christmas the both of you almost ruined brunch with your nonsense."

"Were you Superman?" Stella asked.

"Of course."

Of course.

"Superman can fly and lift buildings," he answered as if that made perfect sense. "Batman has to rely on gadgets."

"Did you have a red cape?"

"Can't be Superman without the cape." He sat back in his chair.

"Tights?"

He shook his head. "It was called a jump-suit."

She couldn't imagine him in tights any more than she could imagine him in nail polish. "Potato-potahto."

"My boys were so cute when they were babies. Blond and snuggly," Naomi continued down memory lane, Christmas brunch apparently forgotten.

Snuggly? Baby boy was snuggly? Stella raised a hand and hid her smile.

Beau saw it anyway. His gaze narrowed but he didn't look angry. "Are you laughing?"

She shook her head.

"I used to dress them in matching sailor suits." Again Naomi sighed. "Remember Michelle Alverson?"

Without taking his gaze from Stella, Beau answered, "No."

"Your prom date from Coronado High School. She's a lawyer. Divorced with a young son." Naomi paused before she added, "We've been chatting."

Beau looked at his mother and reached for his glass. "She lives around here?"

"No. Chicago. We're Facebook friends."

"Facebook? Jesus."

"Watch your language."

"Are you back to picking out china patterns?"

"I'm never far from it, son. All the women I know my age have three or four grandchildren. All I need is one." She held up a finger. "One. I'm not greedy."

Chapter Six

A thin white crescent hung over Tampa while the rest of the new moon hid in the Earth's shadow, blending into the night sky.

It was the perfect moon. A sniper's moon. A dark, brooding moon under which it was difficult to see or be seen. Unless a man was trained by the United States Marine Corps to stalk and lie in wait for an enemy determined to take out his fellow soldiers. Unless a man was trained to note his surroundings and pay attention to things that didn't make sense and detect shapes that didn't belong. And if all that training failed a man, a pair of government-issue night-vision goggles and a day/night scope did the trick.

"No. I can't drive her to Texas. Reuniting long-lost sisters is above my pay grade." Beau paced beside the pool as he spoke into his cell phone. An eight-mile-an-hour wind from the south pushed wavy ripples across the clear surface and brushed Beau's bare chest and arms. Underwater lighting shone on the blue Neptune mosaic tiles and spread onto the concrete deck above. The light wavered across Beau's bare feet as he moved between the spots of light and darkness.

"That's why you're not getting paid," Blake responded.

"I have a job Sunday." Never mind that it was more a business discussion with a buddy and not an actual job. Beau stopped by the steps to the Jacuzzi at one end and looked out at the points of light in the gulf. He'd stripped to a pair of blue swim trunks that hit him mid-thigh. "I have a business to run."

"It's *your* company," Blake said, a slight edge to his voice. "You can take time off if you want." Other people might not detect that edge, but Beau wasn't other people. He'd been competing with his brother since the womb. It was the you-got-a-blue-ribbon-and-I-got-a-red-ribbon edge. It was the I-should-be-happy-for-you-but-I'm-not edge. The edge that crept into their voices when one did better than the other. When one of them was doing a little better in life than the other.

"Your point, sand sailor?" Today it was Beau doing better than Blake. Beau clutching the blue ribbon while Blake held red. Tomorrow things could change.

"You can send someone else, grunt."

"I don't want to send someone else." For the past three years he'd worked his ass off. Mostly because he didn't know a different way of doing things. He was a Junger. Jungers made over-achievers look like slackers.

"Where is this job?"

"New Orleans."

"Lovett is on the way." Blake had obviously been drinking. Again.

"Last time I checked, Louisiana is south of the Texas Panhandle."

"What we've got here is a fluid situation." Since Blake had retired from the teams, he'd been drinking more than usual. There'd been a time when both brothers could drink all comers under the table. It was that whole competition thing. Beau wondered who Blake was competing against these days. "I'd come and get her, but I told Vince I'd stay here and help him out with some last-minute renovations." In the background, Blake popped the top of an aluminum can. "How's Mom?"

Beau let his brother change the subject for now and watched the lights of a sailboat as it slowly drifted past. "Too thin." His mother had always been thin, but she seemed to be thinner than usual. He glanced at the veranda where his mom and Stella had polished off a bottle of wine before heading to bed and presumably passing out. Within the black curtain of a moonless night, the light from the back of the house bathed the stucco arches and columns in soft gold and lit the upstairs veranda in pale shadows. As he talked with his brother about their concerns for their mother's weight, he glanced up at the guest room windows. Well, one of the guest rooms. The windows were dark and reflected the dim light from outside.

"Could be the stress of living with Dr. Mike."

"Could be," Beau agreed. He and his brother knew that when their mother felt stress, she didn't eat. They'd lived with it just as they'd lived with their father's cheating. "I'll talk to Mike." He needed to get off the phone and make a few more calls before he called it a night. But not before he fired his brother up. "Oh. One more thing."

"Yeah?"

"Batman's a pussy."

"Bullshit! Batman is genius and a skilled veteran of ninjutsu. All Batman has to do is shove kryptonite up Superman's ass and he's fucking useless."

Beau laughed as he pictured his brother jumping up in defense of his superhero. "Superman is faster than a speeding locomotive."

"Batman has the Batmobile and Batpod. Both are rigged with grappling hooks and machine guns."

"Superman is the man of steel." Beau smiled in the darkness. "Means he's rigged with a dick of steel. A big dick of steel trumps gadgets any day of the week."

"What good does that do when he only bones Lois Lane?"

"Being a one-woman man isn't a weakness."

"It's kryptonite, man. Kryptonite."

Blake was being a drama queen, but even if monogamy was kryptonite, Beau wanted to give it a try. It had to be better than waking up with a parade of nameless women at the age of thirty-eight. Rather than argue, he got off the phone, then made a few calls. He left a message regarding the change he needed to his itinerary with his operations manager, Deborah, and chatted briefly with his second-in-command, Curt Hill. He'd incorporated Junger Security in Nevada because of the tax and privacy advantages. He had a physical business address in Las Vegas and owned a condo in Henderson, but his work took him all over the country. He was home so little, he didn't really feel at home when he *was* there. Which in turn gave him little time for the social life he'd been meaning to get.

He tossed his phone on a padded deck chair and dived into the deep end of the pool. He might have joined the corps, but he'd spent most of his childhood swimming in anticipation of BUD/S.

He came up for a breath, then started the steady combat stroke his father had taught him. A combination of sidestroke, freestyle, and breaststroke. Pull. Pull. Twist. Breathe and glide. His body sliced through the water as he worked tension from his muscles. With each pull and twist and kick, he relaxed in the comfortable rhythm.

The cool water rushed over his face and body, and he thought of his business in New Orleans with retired gunnery sergeant and scout sniper instructor Kasper Pennington. After Kasper had retired from the corps, he'd returned to his home just outside New Orleans. Instead of sitting back and living off his retirement pay, he'd started his own construction company. He bought and flipped homes for profit, but due to Katrina and the poor economy, he'd expanded his business to include remodel and reconstruction. He employed a lot of former military men and women, whether for just a few months while they adjusted to civilian life before they moved on, or if they stuck around longer. Beau wasn't sure what business discussion Kasper had in mind, but Beau never passed on a good investment opportunity. Could be Kasper wanted some names of guys who needed work. Whether they thought they did or not. His brother came to mind.

After several laps, his thoughts turned to the drive tomorrow. Originally, he'd planned to drive to New Orleans, meet with Kasper, then leave the rented Escalade at the airport and fly home to Nevada for a while.

At the deep end, he flip-turned and swam under water across the pool. His business had grown and he didn't need to travel as much. He'd hired capable people in key positions and his life could settle down now. He could stay at home and start a new phase of his life. One that included a wife and kids. Not because his mother pressured him, but because it's what he wanted.

He broke the surface and pulled oxygen deep into his lungs. He had a lot to think about between now and when he dumped a certain black-haired irritant in Texas. One thing he *didn't* want to think about was Stella laughing it up with his mother. Pulling her hair over one bare shoulder as she and his mother got inebriated. Tanked while sharing a bottle of pinot. He didn't want to think about her smile or the shape of her lips or the things the accidental touch of her arm did to his insides. He didn't want to think of how she looked sitting across the table, the late sunlight tangled in her hair and bathing her smooth skin. He didn't want to think about the curve of her neck or the shadow her chin made on her throat. He didn't want to think of her breathy little moan or her blue eyes looking back at him as she rambled about unicorns and padded bras.

At the wall in the shallow end, he turned and headed back across. No, he didn't want to think of blue eyes and breathy moans and padded bras, but he seemed to be having a harder time controlling his thoughts than usual. No matter the mind tricks he'd used in the past. Earlier, he'd sat at his mother's table, converting wind velocity to minutes of angle in his brain while his body drowned in deep, dark lust. Lust that had finally cooled, not because of his mind-over-body tricks, but because of his mother's talk of Facebook *friends*. He wondered how many of his other old girlfriends his mother had stalked.

He didn't know how long he swam, lost in his thought and paying attention to his muscles rather than counting laps, when he noticed a white blur at the edge of the pool. He stopped in the middle of the deep end where the water reached the top of his shoulders and brushed his hands over his face. Light from within the pool shone up on Stella's bare feet and legs. She wore white. A long shirt maybe. The full-value wind picked up the bottom and it fluttered against her thighs. Beau stared through the outlying shadows and into the umbra shades covering her face.

There were a lot of things he could have said. Could have asked. But the most important seemed to be "What are you wearing?"

She bent forward, and the white shirt slid down her thighs to her knees. "A nightshirt?" she said, her voice was disjointed and soft, like a caress clothed in black velvet. "Your mother lent it to me. She gave me the pants, too, but they're way too long, and I don't like to wear pajama pants to bed anyway." She straightened. "I forgot to pack pajamas this morning."

She hadn't packed anything to sleep in. What would she wear tomorrow night? "Why aren't you asleep?"

"Your splashing woke me up."

"Sorry." He ran his hands over his head. "I'm done. You can go back to bed."

Instead, she knelt by the edge of the pool. "Your mother is a nice woman." The light shone up the front of her shirt, shimmered on the waves, and touched her throat and chin and mouth.

"I know. Surprised?"

"A little." The corners of her lips tilted up. "You're a hard . . . ah . . . ah . . ."

"Ah what?"

"Marine."

Nice save.

"What's the plan for tomorrow?"

"I'm headed to New Orleans." He moved a few steps closer so their raised voices wouldn't wake his mother. "I've got business there."

"Then what?"

"That depends on you. You can either get on a plane or I can take you to Lovett after New Orleans."

She tilted her head in thought and the light brushed across her cheek. "Well, you're kind of crabby, but I don't want to fly to Texas."

"I'm not crabby." Even to his own ears he sounded crabby.

"I guess I'll let you drive me to Lovett," she said through a sigh as if she was doing *him* a favor. As if she had other choices when he got the feeling she clearly did not. "Do I get to meet your brother?"

"If he's still there." She did that thing with her hair. Pulled it to one side so that it looked very black against her white shirt. Her hair curled beneath her breast and did that thing deep in his groin that made him forget she was only twenty-eight.

"Are you the good twin or the evil twin?" She also did the thing with her mouth. Smiled like she thought she was funny.

"I'm the good one." But at the moment, his thoughts headed south toward evil again. He spread his arms wide across the surface as if he was innocent and pushed waves against the edge.

"Or are you really the evil twin masquerading as the good twin?"

He and Blake had been fascinated with twin movies and had seen them all. Not that there were many. "Like *The Other*?"

She shook her head. "Like *South Park*. When Cartman had an evil twin who turned out to really be the good one."

"Jesus." A cartoon.

"Don't tell me you've never seen *South Park*."

"Maybe here and there." While she'd been watching cartoons, he'd been watching high-value targets. He'd been sweating on rooftops in Iraq or freezing his balls off in the Afghanistan mountains, picking off terrorists and making the world a safer place. Sometimes making the mistake of thinking that he really was Superman. "I've been kind of busy."

"Doing spy stuff?"

"Are we back to that?"

She grasped the edge of the pool and leaned forward to brush the surface water with the fingertips of her free hand. "Maybe you're not a spy, but you know stuff about me." She scooped water into her palm and let it run down her fingers and drip into the pool. "I wonder how much you know."

"Not a lot," he answered truthfully. "Other than you got busted for unicorn graffiti." One drop, then two fell from her fingertips into the clear water. "And you shoplifted a padded bra."

"I wish I hadn't told you and Naomi that." She leaned forward a little more and her fingers brushed the ripples in the water. Back and forth, barely skimming the top, teasing the surface.

A shudder tugged at Beau's spine and worked its way to his shoulders, knotting his muscles as he held himself tight. "Yeah" was all he seemed capable of saying. Beau Junger, scout sniper, United States Marine, HOG, reduced to mindless lust.

"I wish you didn't know things about me," she continued, as her hair fell forward and light shimmered in the black strands. "While all I know about you is that you have a killer right hook, you're kind of uptight, and you have a really nice mother. Oh, and you're a Marine. Which isn't a surprise, considering."

He was glad she didn't know things about him.

Glad she didn't know the things her smiles and hair and the sight of her fingers drifting across the water did to him. Glad she didn't know that below the soft, wavering ripples, he was hard as a steel pipe.

She lifted a hand and pointed it at him. "And I also know your mother wants you to start producing kids." She chuckled. "Better get started on that, soldier."

Several drops of water slid down her hand and dripped into the pool. Her soft laughter tugged at the knot in his shoulders and spine and the hard-on in his shorts and all he could think of was that he'd like to get started on that. He'd like to get started on her. "Marine," he said just above a whisper. He'd like to start with her mouth and work his way down. "A soldier is Army."

She flicked a droplet of water at him and laughed. "Potato-potahto."

One second he was looking at her small hand, wet fingers, and soft palm, and in the next he grabbed her wrist and pulled. To stop her laughter and the things it did to him. Because he had no control. Because he couldn't stop himself from wanting her to touch him. Because he'd been thinking about it since she'd accidentally touched him earlier.

The big splash cut her scream short and a wave of water swamped Beau's mouth and chin. She came up gasping through a tangle of wet hair.

"Help," she sputtered, the white shirt floating up her belly.

Beau turned away from the glimpse of bright pink panties and bare legs beneath the surface. He swam toward the ladder on the other side.

"Help!"

No way.

"I can't swim," she gurgled through all that thrashing.

Right.

"Beau!"

He grabbed the ladder and glanced over his shoulder at the flailing white shirt and dark hair. She went back under and his brows lowered. "Quit playing." She wasn't coming up. All she had to do was kick off the bottom and grab the side of the pool. "Stella?"

Her head broke the surface. She sputtered and gave a watery cry before she sank again.

Jesus. He pushed off the side and had her beneath her flailing arms within seconds. They came up in a gush of water and tangled limbs and hair. "I'm drowning," she choked.

"You're fine. I've got you."

"I can't swim."

Clearly. "You're not that far from the side of the pool."

She pushed her hair from her eyes and glanced at the side of the pool several feet away. "Are you trying to kill me?"

The shirt floated just beneath her brushed his belly and chest. He should t Push her to the edge of the pool and let her g just stand there, feeling the cool water and bru of cotton. His voice came out rough, low when he asked, "Why would I do that?"

She looked back at him and her hands settled on his shoulders. "So you wouldn't have to take me to Texas."

Maybe it was the moon and the envelope of darkness. Her lips just below his. Her hands on his skin. His body so close to finally getting what it craved like a junkie craved his favorite drug. He moved a hand to the back of her neck and slid his arm around her waist. He pulled her to him and lowered his mouth to her. Shirt and bare skin pressed into his chest and belly, and a flood of want and need and greed surged through his veins like liquid flame. He felt the breath of her gasp and took advantage of her parted lips. He knew how to kiss a woman to get what he wanted, how to give just enough to make her want him. He was thirty-eight. A man. A man who loved everything about a woman's body. The touch and smell and taste. A man who loved to take his time, but God. God, her mouth was soft. And wet. And tasted good. And he couldn't think beyond her warm mouth and the front of those pink panties pressed into the front of his swimming trunks. Into his erection.

warm mouth a little wider. Her
...ed with his, drawing him a little
...ion got a little tighter, the kiss a
... the world around them a whole

...Mm... moaned as she had during dinner.
A breathy moan of pleasure that made his skin
so tight he ached.

He tangled his fingers in her hair and pulled her
closer. She was good. So good, and he was gone.
Gone. Drowning in her. Drowning in the raw lust
pulsing through his body. Lost in the heat of him
and her. Of their bare bellies touching and that
damn shirt floating all around and keeping her
bare breasts from resting on his chest. So lost he
wanted to push her against the side of the pool and
shove aside the little scrap of her panties covering
paradise. So close he wanted to pull out his cock
and thrust into her. Taking what he wanted.

God he wanted that. Wanted it so much his
hands shook as he pushed her to the side of the
pool. Pushed her and turned away.

Stella touched her free hand to her lips as she
watched Beau climb up the ladder and onto the
deck. Who would have thought he could kiss like
that? Certainly not her. Light slid up his long legs
as water splashed to the concrete from his tall
body and shorts. Without a word or a backward
glance, he walked to one of the chaises and

reached for \
gone, swallowing ~~n the seat. Then he was~~
the house.   by ~~rkness as he moved to~~
She let out a brea
top of her wet head. d mo~~v~~ed her hand to the
she had earlier off a ~~c~~~~u~~lt a l~~i~~ttle buzzed. Like
Only now she was compl~~e~~ of g~~l~~asses of wine.
A door to the house shut a~~s~~ober.
edge of the pool. Consumed. S~~r~~ hand fell to the
yet he hadn't really touched her~~f~~elt consumed,
been something in the air. Some~~l~~. There had
surrounded them. Something in his bl~~a~~that had
cloud that had hit her with relentle~~s~~~~t~~hunder-
Something she'd never experienced before.~~aves.~~

She let go of the edge and sank down into~~.~~
water. She hadn't been thinking about kissi~~n~~
Beau Junger. Hadn't been thinking about him
kissing her, but once he did, she hadn't wanted
him to stop.

The shirt billowed about her as she tipped her
head back and slowly resurfaced. She ran her
hand over her head, smoothing her hair back.
Beau. The kiss. Her reaction. It was all so
confusing. One moment she'd been kneeling by
the edge of the pool on dry ground trying not to
stare at his big shoulders and some sort of black
cord around his thick neck, and in the next, he'd
yanked her into the water. One moment, she'd
been pretending that she was drowning, thinking
that she would get back at him for pulling her

into the water and getting   laugh, and the
ut. One moment,
next, he was kissing her out, and the next,
he'd been kissing he oxic waste.
he'd pushed her away r and hauled herself out
Stella swam to nered her hair over one
of the pool. shed the water out. Stella had
shoulder and sq in her life. She'd kissed men
kissed a lot of ed and men who meant nothing.
she liked a en who'd made her pulse leap with
She'd kiss and attraction, and she'd kissed frogs,
anticipat a prince. She was sort of a kissing
hopin seur, but she'd never experienced anything
con Beau. His kiss had been a complete shock. A
li to the senses. A knock to the head. A surprise
out of nowhere, and she got the unsettling notion
that she'd just been kissed by an expert. A man for
the first time in her life. Which was just crazy.

She gathered the bottom of her shirt and
squeezed. Beau was certainly the oldest man she'd
kissed, but her last boyfriend had been thirty. That
certainly qualified him as a man.

Although Jeremy had been thin enough to fit
into her navy Banana Republic trench coat,
he'd still been a man. And yeah, he'd liked the
coat so much, he'd worn it on more than one
occasion. She usually wasn't into brand names,
but she'd loved that coat and it had
mysteriously gone missing when she'd dumped
Jeremy. Maybe Jeremy had been a little more

metro than male, but he'd still been a man.

Kind of.

She gathered some of the shirt at her hip and squeezed. Just for the sake of curiosity, she wouldn't have minded if the kiss had lasted a little longer. But he'd pushed her away and headed for the house like he couldn't get away fast enough.

A little smile twisted one corner of her lips. He'd wanted her. She'd felt it in his kiss and against her thigh. He'd been hard and ready, but instead of taking things to the next step, or trying to, he'd left. Like he was trying to be noble or decent or something. Like he'd been worried that things would go too far.

Stella sat at the edge of a chaise in the darkness. He needn't have worried. Things would not have gone too far. She would have stopped him.

A slight breeze chilled her skin and cotton shirt. She should go in but she was far too awake for bed. She hooked her heels on the edge of the chair and hugged her knees. She might not have experienced anything like Beau's kiss. She might have wanted more, but she would have stopped. She always stopped. Always. As her abuela told everyone, *Estella es una buena nina.* Perhaps because of the circumstances of her birth, Abuela made sure Estella was a good girl. She didn't swear. Didn't wear red fingernail polish, at least she hadn't until she'd moved out, and she didn't take her shoes off at parties.

121

Stella rested her cheek on her knee. And she didn't have sex before marriage. She was a twenty-eight-year-old virgin by choice. At first she'd remained a virgin out of fear. Fear that her grandmother would take one look at her and know she was one of "those" girls. Out of fear that she'd have a baby like her mother. Even after she moved out and lived in Vegas, her grandmother's cautions and rules still played in her head. In her early twenties, she'd come close to giving it up several times but had always stopped. She'd discovered ways of intimacy while technically keeping her virginity. She knew what some people thought about that. That there was no such thing as a "technical virgin," but she didn't care what other people thought and felt. She was twenty-eight. She'd waited this long, and if she wanted to save sexual intercourse for marriage, she would.

She didn't have a lot. Only herself. She was the only thing that she had to give to the man she would love forever.

Chapter Seven

Stella held her grande caramel macchiato to-go in front of her mouth. The scented steam rose from the small black opening and fogged her sunglasses while a steady *crunch, crunch, crunch* from the other side of the car filled her ears. She'd never seen anyone eat an apple like that. She never knew an apple could be that *loud*. This was not the same man who'd eaten at his mother's table the night before. This was not the man who placed his napkin in his lap and used the right fork. This was a man who ate like he had five minutes to get as much as he could in his stomach. This was a Marine who had three dead apple cores lined up on the console between the leather seats. *Crunch*. His mother was right. He was a hog. Although hearing his nice, polite mother call him out on it was a bit of a shock. Not quite as shocking as watching him hog down his apples, though.

Stella took a sip of her coffee and choked mid-swallow when he hit the window button and tossed one core after another out onto I–10. "You're littering," she pointed out as she wiped a drop of caramel macchiato from her chin. If he made her get a drop of coffee on her white tank top she was going to kill him.

He glanced at her through his mirrored sunglasses, then back at the interstate. "Biodegradable material."

"It's still littering."

He shook his head as he hit the button and closed the window. "Given the heat and humidity and the number of times those cores will be run over, they'll completely decompose in a few days. If not, animals will cart them off."

Her mouth dropped open a little. "You're luring wild animals onto the highway."

His answer was a slight shrug of one big shoulder. His black polo shirt matched his black heart.

"There's probably a law against that."

"Probably." He reached for his own coffee in the cup holder and took a few gulps. "Are you going to make a citizen's arrest?"

She sat back and folded one arm under her breasts. "Of course not. I just don't think you should lure little wild animals to certain death."

"Are you doing that thing where you think you're being funny?"

She frowned. "No." Some things weren't funny. Like certain death for critters.

He laughed and rested his cup on the knee of his khaki cargo pants. "Too bad. You're actually funny this time."

Stella frowned and turned her attention to the highway divided by a grassy median. A forest jam-packed with pine trees bordered each side, and sure enough, on the shoulder lay a sad gray lump. "Look," she pointed out. "A poor little opossum. Lured to its death by irresistible apple cores."

"That isn't an opossum. It looks like a neck pillow."

"Oh." She took a closer look as they whizzed past and hated that he was probably right. Not that she preferred a dead animal, but . . . "Well, littering is tacky, whether it's 'biodegradable material' or pillows."

"Pillow probably just flipped out of the back of someone's truck and they didn't know it until they got home. Now they're screwed because they have a stiff neck and no pillow." He paused, then added, "Of course, it might have seen an irresistible apple core and jumped to certain death."

She looked across at Captain Smartass. "You're unusually chatty this morning."

"You don't know me well enough to know if I'm 'unusually chatty.' "

That was true. "I know you well enough to miss your grumpy side." Which wasn't true.

He glanced at her, then back at the interstate. "I'm not grumpy." He drifted into the right lane and dropped his free hand to the bottom of the leather-covered wheel. "Not usually, at any rate. But you're fairly annoying."

"Me?" She pointed her to-go cup at her chest. "I'm annoying?"

"This can't be news to you." He shoved his own cup into the holder. "Someone has to have told you that before."

"No. I've never met anyone as rude as you."

"You're a bartender. I call BS."

She'd had to put up with some really obnoxious drunks, that was true. "No. You're the rudest person."

"I prefer honest." The corners of his mouth turned up in a slight smile.

"I prefer rude."

"This disagreement is what's called a teachable moment."

She pushed her sunglasses to the top of her head. "Who's supposed to learn something? Me or you?"

"You are, Boots."

"I'm wearing flip-flops."

"Boots is a new recruit." He looked at her and grinned like *he* was really funny. "See what you just learned. Maybe you should call me Staff Sergeant Junger."

"You're a sergeant?" Of course he was.

"First Battalion, Fifth Marines."

She returned his smile. "What were you trying to teach me last night in the pool, Sergeant Junger?"

"Last night was a bad idea." His smile fell and he looked back at the road. "We should forget it happened."

"We should?" He was probably right, but that wasn't likely to happen. At least not for her.

"We're going to be cooped up in this car for a least two more days before I can dump you off in Texas. We don't need complications."

Dump? *Dump!* "Like the complication of your tongue down my throat?"

"You weren't complaining." His frown deepened. "You were moaning."

"I didn't moan."

"You moaned."

Maybe a little. "You groaned."

He glanced at her and she could feel his hard gaze from behind his mirrored glasses. "Let's just forget it happened. Do you think you can do that?"

"It wasn't that memorable." She waved a hand. "It's forgotten."

He looked like he wanted to argue about his memorability, but he returned his gaze to the road and said, "You don't have to worry that it will happen again. It won't."

She knew she should be more relieved than insulted. And she was. Really. If he wanted to forget it happened, fine. She had enough to think about besides the shock of Beau Junger's hot mouth on hers. Like her mess of a life.

After they'd said a quick good-bye to Naomi, they'd jumped in the Escalade and headed to the nearest Starbucks, where she'd been confronted with reality. She didn't have a job and five dollars was a lot for coffee. Beau had paid for the coffee and Naomi had packed apples and croissants for them to munch on, but this trip was going to put a hit on her bank account. A hit she couldn't afford.

Her rent was paid for the month and she did have some money in the bank. Maybe if she was really careful, she'd be okay financially. She'd have to find a new job when she got back, not to mention a new place to live. Stella wasn't worried about finding a new job. She was a damn good bartender and made good tips. She could always find a job.

A new apartment was going to be trickier.

Stella pulled at the legs of her jean shorts and sank further in her seat in an effort to get more comfortable. She figured she had about five days. Two days to get to Texas, two to visit her sister before she flew back to Miami and found a job.

Sadie. She didn't want to think about her sister. Thinking about Sadie made her stomach get all tight and nervous. Thinking about Sadie made her feel like a kid again, sitting at the library, surfing the Internet and the *Amarillo Globe* for news of Clive and her sister. And while she'd hung on every mention of Sadie's 4–H accomplishments, her sister hadn't even known she was alive.

Stella chewed on the inside of her lips and looked out the side window. She'd think about Sadie later. When she was alone. Right now she needed to think about the Gallo boys and Ricky. Did she really need to relocate? Moving to a new city was expensive and she hadn't saved for it. Did she have a choice? Where would she go?

She glanced across at the man who'd help blow her life to hell. He was rude and she'd prefer to ignore him, but she had to know. "Do you really think I need to move out of my apartment? Or were you just being dramatic?"

He looked over at her. "I'm never dramatic and yes. You need to move."

She closed her eyes. "How?" she said, more to herself than to him.

"Hire movers."

She opened her eyes. He made it sound so easy. "I don't have a job. Remember? I can't just hire movers."

"You have a trust fund."

She wasn't even surprised he knew about the trust. Irritated, but no longer surprised. "That isn't my money."

"What do you mean? Of course it's your money."

She shook her head. "It's my mother's money."

"Your father set it up for you when you were born."

The money had never been hers. She didn't even know exactly how much was in it these days, and it was best not to even think about it. "My mother is the trustee."

His brows lowered beneath the silver rim of his sunglasses. "When does it stipulate your age of maturity?"

"Twenty-five or marriage." Which was why at the age of eighteen her stepfather drove her to Vegas and tried to force her to marry his nephew. Carlos and her mother had been divorced for several years, but he'd never given up on the idea of controlling all that money. He just hadn't counted on Stella's refusal to go along with his plan.

"You're twenty-eight," he pointed out needlessly.

She shook her head and pushed away the memory of those few days. Of the drive there and thinking she was going on a fun vacation, only to be locked up in a hotel room with a boy her age who didn't speak English. He'd been even more afraid than she'd been, and he watched her escape out a bathroom window while Carlos slept. She remembered calling her mother and her mother's hurtful response. It had seemed to Stella that Marisol had been more angry than concerned. More angry over the potential loss of the money than concerned for Stella's welfare. "It's my mother's money," she repeated. "She supports herself and Abuela and my other grandparents in Mexico."

"What about you?"

"She took care of me until I was eighteen." Stella might not have had the latest or best of everything, but other people had less. "Then I started taking care of myself."

"Your father put that money in trust for you. You should have gained control of it at twenty-five."

"It's in a joint trust account, now."

"What?" His brows drawn in confusion, he

glanced at her, then back at the road. "How did that happen?"

Stella shrugged. "Guilt." On Stella's twenty-fifth birthday, the day the trust seamlessly settled on Stella and her mother's job as trustee ended, Marisol came to Stella with a folder of documents and a boatload of guilt. How would Marisol and the grandparents live, if not for the money? Did Stella want them all to live in the street? Was she so selfish she'd watch them starve?

She finished her caramel macchiato and put the cup in the holder. "My father never gave a shit about me, and I don't want to talk about his money." It was a useless conversation. Useless to think about all the things she could do with that money or that her father had set up the trust because he cared. "Are the Gallo brothers going to come after me when I go home? Even if I move?"

He dipped his head and looked at a rest stop sign on the side of the road. "Do you want to run into them when you're out and about?"

"Miami is a big city. Maybe they'll forget about me."

He turned on his blinker and merged to the right. "You smashed Lefty Lou's bum hand. Probably broke it. I doubt he'll forget about that."

"You knocked Ricky out and put that flash-bang under the Gallos' car!" Her scalp got a little tingly.

"Exactly."

"They're probably looking for you, too."

"Probably." He pulled into the rest stop.

"What am I going to do, now?"

"Well, I don't know about you, but I have got to piss like a racehorse."

"That's disgusting." Her nose crinkled.

"Sorry." He shoved the vehicle into park and turned the key. "I have to use the *facility* and I suggest you do the same." He took off his sunglasses and tossed them on the dash. "The next stop isn't for another seventy-two miles."

Her life was a scary mess and he was no help except to offer bathroom break info. Without a word, she grabbed her backpack and followed him across the parking lot, past a row of palm trees, to the brick building. Because she wasn't all that certain he wouldn't leave her stranded, she quickly did her business and waited for him outside on a bench next to a big map of Florida behind Plexiglas. Reaching into her backpack, she pulled out her cell and stared down at her blue toenail polish and rubber flip-flops as she dialed.

"Hi Malika," she said when her friend from work picked up.

"Stella! Where are you?"

Maybe her life didn't totally suck. Maybe Ricky had moved on. "About an hour or so north of Tampa."

"What happened Thursday night? Ricky is looking for you."

She guessed not and glanced around as if her former boss might jump out at her. "Why?" she asked, eyeing a family of tourists in matching Disney T-shirts. "What did he say?"

"It's kind of hard to understand him because his jaw is wired shut and his face is black and blue."

Stella gasped. "Oh no." That's why he'd sounded like he was speaking through gritted teeth. He had been.

"Yeah, and that creeper friend of his has his hand all bandaged up. Not the short fat one; the creeper without a thumb. Yuck!"

"Crap."

"They're asking everyone at the bar if we've seen you. Last night, they locked themselves up in Ricky's office, and when Tina took them a bottle of Patron, she said they were watching security tapes from Thursday night."

Oh no.

"They also want to know about some big dude in a black Escalade that you might have met at the bar on Back Door Betty Night. Did you get kidnapped by a drag queen? Should I call the cops?"

"No!" She raised a palm and covered her eyes. "I haven't been kidnapped." Her hand dropped to her lap and she watched Beau walk toward her. Definitely not a drag queen. Without question a big dude. "Ricky is a maniac. Stay away from him."

"What happened?"

"The less you know, the better. I'm going on vacation for a while. I'll call you when I get back. Don't tell anyone you talked to me. Promise."

"Okay."

"I'm serious."

"Promise, geez."

She pressed disconnect and dropped her cell into her backpack. She gave Malika half a second before she was speed dialing everyone she knew. Not that Stella blamed her. She'd totally do the same thing. "You broke Ricky's jaw."

"Right." Beau scoffed as he squinted into the bright morning sun. "I didn't hit him that hard."

She stood and hung her backpack over one shoulder. "I just talked to Malika. She said Ricky's jaw is wired shut and he's asking questions about me and you. They're looking at the security tapes from the other night." Her pulse sped up and she swallowed hard. "What are we going to do?"

Fine lines creased the corners of his gray eyes. "The guy must have a glass jaw. I barely tapped him."

That's what occupied his brain? Not danger? Not foreboding? But how hard he hit Ricky? "It was more than a tap."

"Are you sorry I knocked that putz out?"

She had a bruise on her arm from where Ricky had grabbed her. "No, but I obviously can't go back to my apartment for a long time." She saw spots in front of her eyes and sank to the bench. "My stuff is there. My whole *life*." Her backpack slid down her arm and landed by her foot. "I just bought new bagels."

"Are you okay?"

She didn't have the energy to lie. "Of course not. My life sucks."

"Are you going to pass out?"

Like he cared. "I hope so." She covered her booming heart with one hand. "I hope I pass out and when I wake up, I discover this has all been a hideous dream."

"Nah." He sat next to her, and his big body crowded her space and warmed her skin. "When you wake up, your life will still suck."

She turned her head and looked at him. "That's not funny."

"I know. You've pissed off three mob associates."

Her mouth dropped. "Me? You broke Ricky's jaw and now they're looking for your black Escalade."

"It's a rental. I'm not worried about me." He hit her with his elbow. "You're screwed, though."

The backs of her eyes stung and her vision blurred with tears. She didn't want to cry in front of Sergeant Junger, and turned her face away. He was big and tough and not afraid of anyone.

"Are you crying?"

She shook her head. Maybe he was too stupid to be afraid, but he didn't really strike her as stupid.

"Don't go squishy on me now, Boots. The worst part is over."

"What?" Her voice came out kind of thin. "How can you say that?" From where she sat, at a rest stop north of Tampa, next to a Marine she'd known for only two days, mobsters looking for them, this felt like "worst" to her. Tomorrow didn't look any better than today.

"Yesterday morning had the potential to go sideways, and I didn't have much of a plan B. Believe me, I was relieved when I rolled up and saw you running out of your building like crocodiles were chomping at your tail."

"You looked calm."

"I was calm. Calm and relieved that I didn't have to drag you from the building."

She sniffed and wiped beneath her eyes. "How do you stay so calm?" She'd like to be chill all the time. Like Beau. Not have a racing heart or panic attacks.

"Complete faith in my skills and abilities. Focus under fire. Lots of practice."

She didn't have skills and abilities like Beau. "I can carry a tune and make an excellent martini. I'm calm when I'm on stage singing or tending bar." She shook her head and looked at Beau out of the corners of her eyes. "But those skills and abilities don't come in handy when I'm running from mobsters."

"Just breathe," he advised as if it was easy. "Slow, steady breaths." He stood and cast a shadow over her. "Everything will work out."

"Easy for you to say." She walked beside him toward the Escalade. "You can go home."

"Sometimes home isn't all it's cracked up to be."

Was he talking about his home or hers? "My apartment is small, but I like it."

"You can't do anything about your apartment today. Get your head in order and occupy your mind with something else. Something on deck." He opened the door for her.

She tossed her backpack on the floor and climbed inside. On deck? "Like?"

"Your sister," he suggested, and shut the door. "Think about your happy reunion with her."

Happy reunion? She'd been trying *not* to think of Sadie. Now Mr. Helper put her sister front and center in her brain. Which was just annoying. To add insult to injury, Mr. Helper plugged his Bluetooth into his ear and made business calls for the next few hours, leaving her to her own thoughts. Thoughts like she wished she had more time to prepare to meet her sister. More time to get mentally ready. More time to get her act together. Maybe get her hair cut and have a cute pedicure.

She reached into her backpack on the floor by

her feet and dug around for her cell. While she liked her life, she was aware that on paper she might look like a loser. A slacker. If she had more time, she might sign up for some college classes. Not just photography and pottery classes like last time, but something smart like sociology or psychology. She was already a bartender. It couldn't be that different. She listened to people's problems all the time, and she might be biased, but she thought she gave pretty good advice.

To keep her mind off meeting her sister and looking like a loser, she pulled out her phone and sent a few text messages to friends. She lied and told them she'd had a family emergency and would be out of town. She should probably call her mom and tell her about Ricky, but her mother would just want her to go to Las Cruces and stay with her. She should definitely tell her mom that she was on her way to meet Sadie, but her mom would read too much into it. Want to know all the details, and Stella didn't know any details. She'd call her mom when she actually knew something.

She put in her ear buds instead and played Zuma's Revenge on her iPad. Just north of Gainesville, she forgot she wasn't alone and sang along to "Pumped Up Kicks." She belted out the chorus and really got into the line about running faster than a bullet.

Her ear bud popped out and she grabbed it, only to realize Beau had pulled it from her ear.

"No," he spoke into his Bluetooth, his mouth turned downward at the corners as his steely gaze as he stared into hers. "I'm not a fan of Foster the People, and unfortunately that isn't the radio." He turned his gaze back to the endless highway. "Yeah, just pick out a unit with security cameras."

In Tallahassee, they stopped at a Subway just long enough to use the bathroom and order lunch. Stella ordered a six-inch chicken breast with American cheese while Beau ordered an enormous foot-long with tons of meat and every available veggie. Even jalapeños. Who did that? Health nuts, that's who. Men who took care of themselves and had muscles like Superman.

After scarfing lunch, they climbed back into the SUV and Beau took command of the music and dialed in a heavy metal radio station. Normally, Stella liked all kinds of music. Her tastes were very eclectic, but she could not stand most heavy metal. Slipknot put her into a killing rage and Pantera made her head implode. As she watched his thumbs tap the steering wheel to the heavy beat of Anthrax, she wondered if he took steroids. She doubted it, because while his arms were big, they didn't look roid bloated. Although thick, he had an actual neck between his head and shoulders, and last night she'd felt his erection against her belly and he didn't seem to suffer from shrinkage. Thinking about his lack of shrinkage made her think about her cotton shirt floating about her in the water, brushing her skin, her legs and breasts as he devoured her mouth.

Devoured. That was the word for his kiss. Devoured, then pushed away.

But it was best not to even think about his obvious lack of shrinkage and devouring kiss. Thinking about it stirred a knot of hunger in her stomach and a question in her mind.

Was Superman super in bed? Not that it mattered. She'd stayed a virgin for twenty-eight years and wasn't about to give it up to the sergeant.

To keep her mind off Superman and his super bed, Stella plugged her music back into her ear and dialed in Lady Gaga. She answered a few text messages, then dropped her phone into her backpack, bored out of her mind. She glanced over at Beau, at the strong line of his jaw and profile of his nose and lips. He had a nice mouth. Strong. Devouring. She bet he was good at more than kissing.

She folded her arms across her chest. Obviously bored *and* out of her flipping mind, she looked out the passenger window. She hit the window button and the glass slid down a few inches. Beau had told her she should think about what was "on deck." Like her sister. The wind hit her face and she backed the glass up a few degrees. She hadn't seen a picture of Sadie in a really long time and she wondered if the two of them looked anything alike. Probably not, since they both resembled their mothers.

Her anxiety leaked out her fingertips and she tapped the window button. Tap. Tap. Up. Down. She wondered what Sadie would see when she looked at Stella. Her father's bastard child or a sister? Tap. Tap. Up. Down. Would she see their father's blue eyes or Stella's darker skin? Would she see a white woman or Hispanic? Tap. Tap. Up. Down. Would she see a person who'd never really fit in anywhere no matter how hard she'd tried?

Once again her ear bud was pulled from her ear and Adele's "Rolling in the Deep" was replaced by air racing past and rumbling through the window. The wind vibrated the inside of the SUV and pierced her eardrums with a super high-pitched whistle.

He was back to being grumpy and sent her a frosty stare from the corners of his eyes. Without a word he took control from his side of the car, rolled the window up, and locked it like she was a five-year-old.

Well, she felt as if she was five years old again. Five years old when she had no control over her life.

"When are we stopping for the night?" she asked as she flexed her shoulders.

"I was planning on driving straight through to New Orleans, but I can't take much more."

She knew the feeling. Her butt had fallen asleep just after they'd crossed the Chattahoochee.

Chapter Eight

She was a colossal pain in the ass. An even bigger pain in the ass than he'd first anticipated, and he could not wait to dump her in Texas and bug the hell out.

Beau raised his whiskey on ice to his lips and took a swallow as he pointed to the six of spades on the blackjack table in front of him. He sat at a table inside the Biloxi Hard Rock Hotel and Casino because he hadn't been able to take it anymore.

The female dealer in a maroon blouse turned over a four and Beau sliced his hands across his cards and stayed with twenty. The dealer moved to the next player, in a god-awful flamingo print shirt and slicked back white hair. The guy's wife sat next to him chattering on about the stuffed snapper and crawfish étouffée at a restaurant across the street. Beau lowered his glass. Stella didn't like to fly. She didn't like the bus. She worried about stupid things like apple cores and roadkill. She sang and sighed and played games with irritating sound effects on her iPad. To top it off, she rolled down the window just enough to fill the SUV with a brain-slapping wind and an ear-jabbing whistle. Beau had been through SERE training. Been subjected to simulated prisoner of war camp. Been deprived of food and sleep and pushed to his mental and physical breaking point, but he didn't recall being as tortured by three days of POW camp as he'd been by spending one day confined with Stella Leon.

The dealer dealt the house a twenty-one and Beau lost a stack of orange and black chips. Around him, the bells and whistles and bloops of slot machines filled the floor. Beau slid another three hundred and fifty into the betting square. As far as he was concerned, slots were for amateurs and old ladies. It took no skill, no strategy to play slots. Just a willingness to sit in the same chair and hit a button.

The dealer slid Beau an ace of clubs and the queen of hearts. She paid out and he let the chips ride. He lost the next round and rolled his neck from side to side as the dealer scooped off his seven hundred in chips and moved to the next player. It didn't seem to be his night. He slid several black and orange chips into the square. Hell, it didn't seem to be his week. He was stuck with a woman who'd found the sweet spot of torture and managed to look innocent and hot as she hit it over and over again. That was the real secret weapon in her torture toolbox. The curve of her neck and waist and ass. One moment he was wondering how he could get her into a sleeper hold while driving down the interstate, and in the next, she flexed and squirmed in her seat and he envisioned her squirming against him. One second he'd been wondering how to bring the boom down on her, and in the next, she brought it down on his crotch.

He'd planned to drive straight through to New Orleans and meet with Kasper tomorrow afternoon. He could still make the meeting, but he'd had to stop. He'd had to get away from Stella. If just for a while. He'd left her in the two-bedroom suite, fussing about cost. He'd tried to explain that certain hotels comped rooms for Junger Security or at least gave corporate discounts, but he didn't think she'd heard him over her fretting.

Beau drained the Gentleman Jack from his glass. The eighty-proof whiskey warmed his throat and stomach and reminded him he hadn't eaten since around noon. The bells and whistles and bleeps and bloops from the slot machines filled his ears as a cocktail waitress in a tiny black outfit replaced his drink. He slipped her a twenty-dollar chip and slid his bet into the square on the table. He wouldn't call himself a big drinker. Not like Blake or his father, but he did like to tie one on every now and then. Tonight felt like a now-and-then night.

He took a drink and felt the burn. He thought of

Stella and money, or rather her lack of money. She had a trust fund she obviously didn't consider hers, and he wondered if her father had known that the money hadn't gone to her. He wondered if her father had cared. She'd said he never gave a shit about her, and it appeared she was right. Although he couldn't imagine having a little girl and not being involved in her life. Not caring what happened to her. A tiny ember of anger burned right next to the whiskey in his stomach. Beau had seen a lot of horrible things in his life. He'd seen a lot of it up close and personal or through the crosshairs of a fixed scope. There were a lot of adults who deserved the horrible things that happen to them. People who asked for it because they were brutal thugs, but kids were different. Kids didn't ask to be born into a war zone or to have shitty parents. They didn't deserve to be disposable or forgotten.

Beau pointed to the ten of diamonds and three of hearts in front of him. He was dealt a five and held at eighteen. He took a drink of his Gentleman Jack as the dealer moved to the guy in the flamingo shirt. Stella had said that her father hadn't given a shit about her, and given that Sadie had never been told about Stella, he had to agree. Sure, Stella could be annoying and a pain in the ass, but that did not excuse Clive Hollowell for loving one child while ignoring the other.

The dealer drew twenty and scooped away

Beau's chips. Well, shit. The whiskey was doing a nice job of giving everything a warm cheery glow. Which was not a good sign. It was a sign that his judgment was impaired. A sign that he should take his remaining chips and bug out. But of course he didn't. Not until he lost his last two thousand in chips.

He downed the last of his whiskey and tipped the dealer his last chip, He stood as sirens and flashing lights split the air. At first, Beau thought the cops were raiding the place and he turned around expecting to see some sort of takedown. A group of gray-haired ladies crowded around a row of dollar slots and one of the machines making all the commotion. Beau moved toward the crowd on his way to the concierge desk. He needed to find a thick steak and a baked potato. The closer he got, the more annoying the flashing lights. A granny had hit pay dirt and probably won enough for her and her friends to party at the buffet. Big deal.

"Holy frijole y *freakin'* guacamole!"

Beau stopped in his tracks and looked through the crowd, catching a glimpse of a familiar white tank top and shiny dark hair. Her fists pumped the air and she danced around like a prizefighter.

"I never win anything!"

A smile cracked Beau's mouth as he glanced around the crowd surrounding Stella. Some grinned and congratulated her while a few were pinch-mouthed and gave her the evil glare. He laughed and moved toward her. That was Stella. Winning some friends and annoying others.

"Beau!" She spotted his face above the crowd; maybe it was the booze or that he was getting older, slower, but before he knew quite how it happened, her arms were wrapped around his neck and his arms were around her waist. Her toes dangled above the casino floor and her front was smashed against his. "I hit the jackpot!"

He felt a hot, lusty tumble low in his stomach and his head spun. And once again before he even thought it through, he planted a kiss on her soft, smiling lips. A kiss that lingered a little past friendly. "Congratulations, Boots." It was the booze. Definitely the booze.

She grinned at him and he felt it next to the tumble in his stomach, the spin in his head, and the hard-on in his pants. And just like the other night in the pool, everything narrowed and focused on her. Her blue eyes and soft mouth. The weight of her hands on his shoulders and the touch of her breasts pressed to his chest. Everything around him blurred except Stella, and he fought the demand of his lust. The demand that he lower his face to hers again. To feel her mouth against his and touch his tongue to hers.

"I've never been this lucky."

He set her on her feet and dropped his hands to

his sides even as his body demanded he grab her and *show* her lucky.

Seventeen thousand dollars. After federal, state, and a three percent gaming tax were all deducted from Stella's Lucky Seven winnings, she was left with just over seventeen thousand dollars.

"I never win anything," she said as she filled out the tax forms. She repeated her amazement as she got her picture taken with an oversize check for the casino's Web site. She was still in shock an hour later as she sat in the padded leather booth at Ruth's Chris Steak House inside the Hard Rock Casino. The tables were covered in white linen and set with china. A white linen napkin rested in Stella's lap and she felt completely underdressed in her tank top and shorts. But one of her sundresses was dirty, and the other wrinkled.

A pretty blond waitress set a plate filled with a lobster tail and asparagus in front of her, and she leaned back against the tall booth. "Thank you," she said as she watched the woman set a T-bone and huge baked potato in front of Beau.

"Can I get you two anything else?" the waitress asked them, but her attention was focused on Beau.

He looked up and gave the woman a smile Stella had certainly never seen before. It creased the corners of his eyes, and if she didn't know him, she'd think maybe his smile was charming. "I'm good. Thank you, Sarah."

"Okay, hon. Let me know if you need anything at all."

Hon? Stella watched the woman walk away and wondered what she saw when she looked at them. A handsome guy with a charming smile, and a woman in a tank top with hair that could probably benefit from a brush. She turned her attention to Beau across the table. "Do you know her?"

He shook his head and picked up his fork and big steak knife. "She's wearing a name tag."

Not that she cared what a woman she didn't know thought of her, but she could buy some new clothes now. She smiled as she thought of the money she'd won. "I never win anything." She picked up her own fork and knife, but she wasn't all that hungry due to her excitement and the huge sandwich and chips they'd had for lunch.

Beau swallowed a big bite of his potato and washed it down with his second glass of ice water. "You've said that about fifty times now."

"I know." She couldn't stop grinning. She'd been freaking out about how she was going to pay for an expensive hotel room that was bigger than her apartment in Miami. A heck of a lot fancier, too, with the enormous windows looking out at the gulf, two cushy bedrooms, and bathrooms with jet tubs and six heads in the three-person showers. Before she'd plugged five dollars in the Lucky Seven slot machine, she worried about how she was going to pay for a Diet Coke from the wet bar. "Now I can pay my half for the room and chip in for gas." And not have to freeload off her sister or anyone else.

"I told you not to worry about it." He set the glass back on the table and cut off a hunk of steak. He'd been drinking, and not just water. Not that it really showed in obvious ways, but she was a bartender and picked up on it. He was just more relaxed. Less uptight. Loose, and of course she'd smelled whiskey on his breath when he'd planted that kiss on her downstairs. "You're a business write-off, Boots."

He'd said that, yes. She still wanted to pay her own way. Buy a swimsuit and a bikini wax if she needed one and not have to worry about how she was going to get home. Or where she was going to live. "I can hire someone to move my stuff from my apartment now."

He raised his gray gaze to hers as he chewed. "I took care of that. I'll need your key so my guys don't have to pick your lock."

A soothing piano concerto played through the restaurant's sound system, and the clank of plates gathered from the next table filled the air. "When?"

"We'll FedEx it tomorrow."

She shook her head and dunked her lobster into butter. "When did you 'take care of that'?"

"Today." He took a bite and swallowed before he continued. "Around the time you were annoying me with 'Pumped Up Kicks.' "

No man had ever taken care of anything for her in her life. "Thank you." It felt strange, she thought as she ate her buttery lobster. New. Different, and she didn't know whether she liked it. "I'll pay for it all, of course."

He shrugged. "It's not that big a deal. I know some guys who owe me." He dug into his potato, and normally the amount of food he ordered would have been an obvious sign of intoxication, but for Beau it was just another meal.

She took a bite and tried not to moan. Beau didn't like it when she moaned, but the lobster was delicious. Technically, she supposed, this was the third time he'd helped her. The first time had been the night he'd punched Ricky. The second, when he'd rescued her from her apartment amid a fog of flashbang. She was afraid she could get used to having a man around who had her back. "You don't like 'Pumped Up Kicks'?" she asked so she wouldn't have to think how nice it felt to have a man pick up a bit of her load.

He swallowed and reached for his water. "Last time I was on Fremont Street, it was playing in all the casinos."

"Fremont Street, Las Vegas?"

His eyes met hers over the bottom of the glass, then he set it back on the table. "Yeah."

"When were you there last?"

"On Fremont?" He shrugged, then turned his attention to his dinner. "About a year ago when I moved to Henderson."

"You live in Henderson, Nevada?"

"Yeah."

"I used to live in North Vegas. In a real crap apartment with two other girls." She laughed and reached for her own water. "We started a girl band. The first of several that I belonged to." She shook her head. "Lord, but I've sung in some real dive bars."

He looked up but he didn't bother to look surprised.

"But you know that. Don't you?"

"I know your employment history." He waved his steak knife in her direction. "And before you get twisted about all that again, you know my employment history as well."

She pulled her hair over one shoulder and stabbed some asparagus. "I only know that you were in the military and now you're a spy." She took a bite and smiled.

Predictably, his brows lowered. "I was in the Marines and I'm not a spy, but I think you know that."

Yeah, she knew that. "Did you drive a tank?" She could see him driving a tank through clouds of smoke and fire and flashbang.

He chewed slowly as he ate, as if he was

weighing exactly what he wanted to tell her. "I was a scout sniper."

Sniper? "Ah, that sounds kind of spy-ish."

"Snipers aren't tasked with gathering that sort of intel."

She guessed she didn't have to ask what he was "tasked with." She looked across the table at him; at the faint candlelight flickering across the contours of his handsome face and shining in his blond hair like a saint's halo. Saint. Superhero. Marine sniper. Security specialist. "How long were you in the Marines?"

"Seventeen years. I entered the corps at eighteen. Right out of high school."

The more she knew of Beau, the more she realized she didn't know him at all. "When I was young I wanted to be a ballerina one year and a nurse the next." After high school, she'd still not had a clear idea of what she wanted to do when she grew up. Still didn't. Two couples dressed for dinner were shown into the next booth. Stella waited for them to pass before she asked, "Did you always want to be a Marine?"

"No. I always thought I would be a Navy SEAL like my father." He took a drink, and a drop of water fell from the bottom of the glass onto his black shirt. He set the glass down and said, "I joined the corps to piss him off."

"Did it work?"

"Oh yeah. He wanted his sons to be SEALs like

him. He hates the Marines and is still pissed at me about it."

"Do you talk to him?"

"When I have to." He shook his head and sliced his meat. "We never did get along."

She looked at his big shoulders and thick neck and square jaw while they ate. There was a scar on the back of one big hand. "Maybe you should have been an accountant."

He actually laughed at her little joke. Okay, not a real laugh. More like an amused ha! "By the time Blake and I were fourteen, we were already expert marksmen and first-class swimmers. It just made sense that I join Marine RECON and apply to scout sniper school."

Of course it did. "So is Batman a SEAL?"

"Blake?" He nodded and took a bite from a big roll. "He was a SEAL sniper. Served his full twenty."

Two snipers? Which begged the question, "Who's the better shot?"

Beau pointed the roll at his chest. "I'm the HOG."

His mother had called him that the night before, and while he ate like each meal was his last, she wouldn't go that far. "You're a healthy eater." She looked up at the booth wall just above his head and thought a moment. If he was worried about it, a gentle critique might help. She returned her gaze to his and said as diplomatically as possible,

"You do eat kind of fast, and I'd hate to get in your way if you're truly starving, but I wouldn't call you a hog. I mean, you're not messy and you don't chew with your mouth open or anything disgusting like that."

He stared at her as he chewed. "H-O-G," he spelled out slowly. "Hunter of Gunmen."

"Oh."

He reached his free hand inside the collar of his shirt. "My HOG's tooth."

He pulled out a bullet on the black cord she'd noticed last night. "It looks like a copper bullet."

"Copper with a steel core. A seven-six-two boat tail."

Which meant nothing to her, and she asked what she thought was the obvious question, "Why is a HOG's tooth a bullet and not a tooth?"

He finished the roll and chewed, again watched her as if he was weighing his words. "I got it when I graduated scout sniper school," he said after he swallowed. "It represents the one bullet that is meant for me, and as long as I have it, no enemy sniper has a bullet with my name on it."

"Like you're invincible?"

"Not invincible. No." He cut off a piece of steak. "But I'm here. Sitting in this fine restaurant with you instead of laid out in Arlington."

The thought of him in Arlington disturbed her. A lot. And that confused her. More than it should. "Your luck must have rubbed off on me tonight," she said, purposely changing the subject. She still couldn't believe she'd won seventeen thousand dollars.

"You feeling lucky, Boots?"

She smiled. "And it's about time I got lucky, too."

He raised a brow, and one corner of his mouth curved up as he chewed.

"Not that kind of lucky." She laughed and pushed her hair behind her ears. "Which reminds me. I thought you weren't ever going to kiss me again."

His chewing slowed and he swallowed. "Are you talking about what happened in the casino?"

"Yeah."

"That wasn't really a kiss."

It had felt like a kiss to her. Not like the other night, but for one brief second, the sound and excitement of the casino ceased to exist. She'd seen him. Only him and his gray eyes looking back at her. Then he set her on her feet and everything came crashing back. "What would you call it?"

"I'd call it a momentary loss of judgment due to Gentleman Jack."

Blaming it on whiskey irritated her. "You put your lips on mine. I call that a kiss."

His gaze slid to her mouth. "It was more like a peck."

"Like you'd give a sister?"

"I don't have a sister."

"Your mother?"

He raised his gaze to hers. "I don't kiss my mother on the mouth."

"Random women in casinos?"

"Depends on the random woman." He shrugged a big shoulder and turned his attention to his dinner. "Are you going to get it all twisted and think it meant something?"

Now he'd just irritated her further. "I don't get things twisted, and I don't think it meant anything other than you can't resist me." *There. Take that, Sergeant.*

He scowled at his plate. "I can resist you."

"Obviously."

"Jesus." He glanced up at her. "It isn't like I put my mouth anywhere interesting or threw you down and laid pipe on the casino floor."

She cocked a brow, leaned closer, and said just above a whisper, " 'Laid pipe'?"

"Go to the bone yard. Ride the baloney pony. Have wild monkey sex." He waved his fork in her direction. "Whatever."

"There was never any danger of that happening on the casino floor or anywhere else." She sat back but kept her voice low. "I'm not going to have sex, monkey or pony or whatever, with you or any man."

His gaze slid to her lips and throat. "Are you a lesbian, Boots?"

"No. I'm just not having sexual intercourse until I am married."

"You're shitting me."

"No."

The blond waitress approached and asked if they needed anything. Beau waited for her to walk away before he said, "You've never had a boyfriend?"

"Of course I've had boyfriends. Doesn't mean I had sex with any of them."

His eyes got kind of squinty. "Is this one of those jokes that you think is really funny but isn't?"

"No."

He lowered his chin and stared into her eyes. "You're saying you're a virgin."

She glanced about to see if anyone had heard. "That's what 'I'm not having sexual intercourse until I am married' means."

He looked skeptical. "Maybe."

She laid down her fork and lifted her hands, palms up. "What else could it possibly mean?"

He ate a few bites before he answered. "It could mean you've had way too much sex."

What? She dropped her hands to the table. "I'm twenty-eight."

"Could mean you've had so much sex that it's just meaningless now. It could mean you've had sex on every continent, and faces and names are just a blur."

She'd never been out of North America and was pretty sure he wasn't talking about her anymore. "That would make me a raging slut."

"I don't know about 'raging.' " He glanced up, then back at his steak. "I wouldn't say 'raging.' "

"What would you say?"

"That you need to sit on the bench for a while until sex means something."

Now it was her turn to be skeptical and she pushed her half-eaten dinner aside. "Are you saying you're on the bench?"

He didn't answer.

"I find that hard to believe."

"And I find it hard to believe that you've had boyfriends but you're still a virgin."

Again she glanced about to see if anyone heard him. "It's true."

"Are you a tease, then?"

She shook her head. "When I get into a relationship, that's one of the first things I let him know."

He continued to eat and asked between bites, "How many relationships have you been in?"

"Three." She thought a moment. "Well, there was that horrible one, so three and a half." He'd been a real player and a jerk. He'd worn biker boots and ski goggles in the summer, and for some reason, she'd thought he was cool. "We didn't go out very long."

He took a drink of water and sucked a drop

from his bottom lip. "Probably didn't like permanent blue balls."

"There are things people can do that don't involve intercourse, you know."

"Yes. *I* do know. There are a lot of things." He cocked his head to one side and set the glass on the table. "What specifically are *you* talking about?"

She'd never before talked about sex with a man she had no intention of having sex with. "Touching and kissing." But what the heck. She checked to make sure the waitress was across the restaurant and said just loud enough for him to hear, "All over."

Slowly he straightened his head. "Oral sex?"

"Yes."

He sat still for several seconds before he resumed eating. "Oral sex is still sex."

She shrugged. "It's not intercourse."

"Someone could argue that a man's mouth between your legs is more intimate."

Her eyes widened and she felt a tight knot pull low in her abdomen. "Maybe." She resisted the urge to look around again. "I don't know. All I do know is that it's mine to give a man, and I want that man to be someone I love and who loves me, too."

A crooked smile tugged at one corner of his lips. "Love and marriage?"

"Yes."

"How long did you end up dating those three and a half boyfriends?"

"Not all that long." If he wasn't embarrassed by the turn in conversation, neither was she. Of course, he always had the excuse that he was drunk and she wasn't. "Men like to get but don't like to return the favor. If you know what I mean."

He paused long enough in his eating to ask, "Says who?"

"Me." She reached for glass of water and took a drink. "Men are more eager at get than give." She set the glass back on the table and brushed the red lipstick near the rim.

"You've obviously been with the wrong men," Beau said as he watched her thumb wipe the lip print.

"One of my boyfriends was okay at it."

"Okay?" He glanced up and his eyes looked a deeper gray than before. "A man can be okay at basketball or matching his pants and shirts. He should never be 'okay' at oral sex. Sex is pretty much our most important job. It's the one thing we have to nail—so to speak—so we get invited back for more. It's pretty much the reason we take a shower and brush our hair."

She fought the urge to squirm in her seat, but the hot little knot in her stomach slid lower. While she was getting all hot and tingly, he didn't appear all that affected by their conversation. He actually picked up the pace and ate faster. God, did he go at sex like he did mealtime? All intense and ravenous? "Well, ah . . ." And why did she find it so hot, and why was she thinking of sex with Beau at all? Definitely not a good idea. "That hasn't been my experience."

"Then you've been with boys not men. I like everything about women. The smell of a woman's neck and hair and where you all put perfume on your wrists. I like the weight of a woman's breasts in my hands and the softness of her skin against mine. I like a woman's moan in my ears." He shoved the last bite of his steak into his mouth, then lifted one hip and pulled his wallet from his back pocket. "I love a pair of warm thighs and the taste of a woman in my mouth. Especially if the woman is as into it as I am." He stood and threw a hundred-dollar bill on the table. "Now if you'll excuse me, I got a date with a cold shower or the porn channel. I haven't decided which. Maybe both."

Chapter Nine

Beau took off his beige ball cap and reached for a discarded T-shirt on the downed cypress tree. The New Orleans temperature hung at eighty-five while the humidity had dropped from that morning's high of ninety percent to a livable sixty-four. Beau wiped sweat and sawdust from his face and the back of his neck. "I should have known this was your work proposition," he said to the man with the chain saw.

Gunnery Sergeant Kasper Pennington laughed and cut the small engine. He set the chain saw on the cypress stump and reached inside a cooler. "You probably wouldn't have come." He grabbed two bottles of ice-cold water and tossed one to Beau.

Beau caught it mid-air and unscrewed the top. His friend and fellow HOG was likely right. For the past few years, he'd been too busy building his business to take time and hang out with buddies. Being with Kasper reminded him that he needed to make the time. Even if it was just cutting down trees. "I finally got to see this house of yours," he said before he raised the bottle to his lips and guzzled half. Beau had logged a lot of hours tipping back whiskey or holed up in a shelled-out building waiting for action, with nothing to do but listen to Kasper go on about home. The two-hundred-year-old plantation house that had been in Kasper's family since before the Civil War. The place had been one of the South's leading sugar producers, but now the big home sat on five acres of mostly overgrown cypress and kudzu. Kasper talked about it more than either of his wives or his string of girlfriends.

"Esterbrook isn't my house. It's my home." Kasper took a drink and looked at Beau over the bottom of the bottle. His brown eyes squinted against the bright afternoon sun, and sawdust and bark chips covered his Cooter Brown's Tavern T-shirt. "You don't understand," he continued after he'd swallowed, "because you were brought up a Navy brat and moved around."

The Jungers had moved around, but even if Beau had been raised in one place all his life, he doubted he'd look at the old house with its massive columns and wraparound galleries as anything but a dinosaur around his neck. "All I can say is that it's lucky for you that you own your own construction company and can afford this money pit."

Kasper raised several fingers off his water bottle. "Three," he said. "Three construction companies. Commercial, new home, and remodel and restoration." He swatted at an insect buzzing around his head. "You're right about the money pit part." Earlier Kasper had shown him around the ten-thousand-square-foot house, parts of it restored while the other parts needed attention. "But worth every cent. Growing up at Esterbrook was amazing. I crawled under acres of kudzu and shot a lot of squirrels around here." Later, he'd crawled in a ghillie suit and shot enemy combatants. He pointed to an overgrown field behind the house. "Some of the old slave quarters are over there. Just dangerous piles of wood now days, but I crawled all over them as a kid," he continued, and pointed out lumps and piles of brick here and there that had once been part of the working plantation. He sounded all nostalgic and shit, which might have been embarrassing for the guy if he wasn't a six-foot-four-inch solid wall of hardened Marine muscle. "Esterbrook survived wars and hurricanes, although we did have some flood damage from Katrina."

The sun's rays cut through the humidity and toasted Beau's face and bare shoulders, and he upended the bottle over his head while Kasper talked about other restoration projects he'd taken on after the storm. The cold water ran down Beau's face and shoulder before flowing down his bare back and chest. The icy water raised bumps on his arms. A lot like the shower he'd taken the night before. *After* he'd watched porn.

As if he'd read his mind, Kasper said, "Tell me more about this little gal you're traveling with."

She was a virgin. Beau raised his free hand shoulder level. "About this tall. Dark hair. Blue eyes." He told Kasper about Back Door Betty Night, Ricky De Luca, and Stella's exfiltration amid the chaos of flashbang. They had a good chuckle over Stella smashing a mobster's hand in her door, because that was funny shit, and they did have an appropriate sense of humor. Unlike Stella.

"How old is this gal?"

"Twenty-eight."

Kasper lifted one black brow. "Young."

"Too young."

"Nah."

She was a virgin. How was that possible? She wasn't ugly or stupid. Although ugly and stupid never stopped some men. The guy in front of him was a perfect example.

"Pretty?"

Beau reached for his shirt and pulled it over his head. "Yeah." Beautiful. Beautiful and young. And a virgin. Technically. Although a case could be made that oral sex was sex. Having a man's penis in a woman's mouth was as intimate as having it in her vagina. Having her red lips wrapped tight around—Beau stopped that train of thought and where it was leading him, but not before desire tugged at his belly. He looked off in the distance at a paddleboat slowly chugging up the Mississippi River. Tourists crammed the decks, and he picked out a spot of red on the port side. Probably a man's hat. If he had his scope, he could sight in the lettering, dial in the dope, and decide where to put the crosshairs above center mass.

"Have you charmed her pants off yet?"

Beau frowned and tossed the empty bottle back into the cooler. So much for calculating MOS. "No. She's a buddy's future sister-in-law." He'd tried *not* to charm her pants off. He'd tried to be stone cold. Except for those two times. When he'd kissed her. "It's not like that."

"You're a man. She's a woman. It's always like

that." Kasper reached for the chain saw. "The Quarter is very romantic. *Laissez les bon temps rouler*," rolled off his Cajun tongue just before he fired up the small engine.

No, there would be no good times rolling with Stella. In the Quarter or anywhere else. Earlier, he'd checked them into the Bourbon Orleans and headed out to Kasper's. He'd left her in the middle of the lobby with her duffel at her feet and a room key in her hand. After last night's conversation, he'd had to get the hell away from her.

No, there would be no good times. Rolling or lying or standing up. Not in a pool or on a casino floor. No good times with her mouth on him and his mouth eating her up. That was not going to happen, but he did wonder what kind of idiots she'd dated in the past. What kind of idiot failed at his job? Making women moan and call out to Jesus wasn't that hard.

Beau shoved his work gloves onto his hands and motioned for Kasper to give over the saw. It was his turn to chew up some Louisiana cypress and keep his mind focused on something other than a certain dark-haired virgin. Focused on his first cut to make sure the tree fell precisely forward. Focused on the danger at hand rather than the danger that waited for him at the Bourbon Orleans later.

Beau pulled the starter rope and set his feet against the tug of the saw's teeth biting into the tree. God, he needed to dump Stella off in Texas, ASAP. Before he doubled over due to relentless blue balls.

The first thing Stella did with some of her Lucky Seven winnings was shop for clothes and a pair of jeweled flip-flops. For a few insane moments, she actually thought of buying cowgirl gear: Wranglers, fringe, boots, and a belt with a huge sparkly buckle. But none of it felt like her, and she went mostly bohemian instead. Boho was kind of cowgirl. Okay, more country than cowgirl, and she did buy a blue plaid shirt to wear with a jeans skirt, but her favorite purchase of the day was a paisley dress she'd found at Saks on Canal Street. It was made of thin gauzy material with a white slip underneath. It was delicate and made her feel pretty.

She bought panties and two bras, and she caught herself looking through lingerie. Slinky, sexy nighties with sheer lace. The kind of nighties no one actually wore long enough to sleep in, and while she looked at the tiny panties and snappy garters, she thought of Beau. Of his mouth and the things he'd said last night. About the things he liked about women. She'd been thinking about the things she'd like him to do to her.

Which of course was ridiculous and embarrassing. She'd known the guy for only four days, counting the night he knocked out Ricky.

Stella opened the door to the third floor suite and stepped inside. A bellman followed and set her shopping bags on the couch. She tipped him ten dollars and slipped her backpack into a gold-and-black striped chair. Except for double doors leading to the intricate wrought-iron balcony, the suite was surprisingly modern. Especially considering the age and the French Creole architecture of the rest of the hotel.

As soon as the door shut behind the bellman, she moved to center of the main floor and glanced up to the loft.

"Hello?" she called up. "Beau?" She listened but didn't hear anyone. She hadn't seen him since he dumped her with a bellman that morning, and it was after six now. He'd mentioned something about visiting a military buddy and apparently hadn't returned.

She moved past the wet bar to the couch and gathered her six bags. She headed up the stairs with six corded handles on each arm. The upper level had a narrow bathroom with black granite and tile and a glass-enclosed shower, and a bedroom with two queen beds. She set the bags on the bed with her duffel and eyed the other. She wondered if Beau knew the suite's sleeping arrangement. She thought of looking over at him during the night and felt a little stitch in her stomach. Too intimate, and someone was going to have to sleep on the couch. Since Beau was big and the couch wasn't, she figured that someone was going to be she.

Stella stepped out of her flip-flops and reached into her duffel. She pulled out a clean pair of white panties and a wrinkled pink sundress and laid them on the bed. She'd certainly slept in worse places than on a couch inside a five-star, luxury hotel. A sleeping bag in a van or a sleazy motel came to mind.

Stella checked her cell phone. She'd had calls from her mother, Ricky, and her dentist's office reminding her she had an appointment tomorrow. She left a message with the dentist's voice mail canceling her appointment and dialed her mom.

"Hi Mom. What's up?" she asked, and sat on the end of the bed.

"Abuela got a jump in her left eye."

Stella got a pain in her forehead. She couldn't keep track of all her grandmother's superstitions. "Maybe it's old age."

"She said you're in trouble. Are you?"

"Well, not really . . . but . . . I'm meeting with Sadie." It still sounded weird to say it out loud.

"Your sister? When? How did that happen? Why didn't you tell me?"

"I'm meeting her tomorrow or the next day." She got more comfortable on the bed and started at the beginning. Well, kind of the beginning. She left out Ricky and the Gallo brothers. She didn't want her mother to worry or Abuela's eye to jump out of her head. "So I'm just chilling in New Orleans tonight and heading to Texas in the morning. It's a little over seven hundred miles so I don't know if we'll make it all the way."

"Who is this man you're with? I don't like you traveling with a man you don't know."

"I told you. His name is Beau and he's a friend of Sadie's fiancé. We stay in different rooms when we stop." Except for tonight. "He's fine, Mom." In more ways than one.

"You don't know him to say that. Only four days."

It felt like longer. Maybe because they'd spent so much time together, but it felt like she'd known him weeks, months, maybe longer. How long did it take to know a man well enough to know the way he walked and talked or sat in stony silence? How long to know that his rare smiles reached the corners of his eyes? How long to know the way he ate? Like he had so little time and so much to chow. How long to know the touch of his hand and the way his shoulder felt beneath her palm? How long to know his eyes turned a deeper shade of gray when he looked at your mouth? How long to know the touch of his mouth made your insides feel all squishy? "He's a retired Marine sergeant, Mom. He's safe." How long before you knew you wanted to feel more?

"Give me his phone number in case something happens and I can't contact you."

Right. "He's not here right now. I haven't seen him all day." She failed to mention she had his business card and his number saved in her phone.

"Did he leave you stranded in New Orleans?"

"No." He hadn't left her stranded at her apartment or at MIA or dumped her at his mother's or at the Hard Rock. "He's helping out a friend. He'll be back." She glanced at the clock. It was almost seven. "I'll call you when I get to Texas."

"Are you worried?"

For all that her mother had her faults and certainly drove Stella crazy, she also knew her. "About Sadie?"

"Yes. She will love you, Estella."

She swallowed and said through forced laughter, "Of course she will. To know me is to love me."

"Don't joke. I think this is all a sign."

The pain in Stella's forehead spread. "What sign?"

"We'll have to wait and see. It's Father's Day."

It was Father's Day? Shopping today, she'd seen the Father's Day signs in stores but hadn't paid enough attention to make the connection.

"Perhaps it's a sign from Clive that he finally wants his girls to meet."

Doubtful. "I'll call you."

"Soon."

"Okay." Father's Day was just another day to her. "I love you, Mom."

"Te quiero, Estella."

172

Stella hung up the phone and tossed it on her bed. She grabbed her shampoo and conditioner and headed for the bathroom down a short hall. Today was just another Sunday. Like all the other Father's Days in her twenty-eight years. It was nothing to her.

She stripped off her clothes and jumped into the shower. Warm water ran down the sides of her head and back and she closed her eyes. When she'd been told that her father was dead, she'd had little reaction. A man who didn't want to know her didn't deserve a reaction.

Behind her closed lids, the backs of her eyes stung like she was going to cry or something. Cry for a man who never cried for her? For a father who never wanted to be her father?

Why now? Why was she suddenly feeling all weepy and emotional? Why today instead of the day she'd learned of his death? Maybe because hearing from Sadie had dug at the old hurt in her soul. The hurt she'd patched over long ago, but after four days of relentless picking, she suddenly ached with old and familiar "what ifs" and "if onlys." With childish hopes and forgotten dreams. Hopes and dreams of a warm and fuzzy future that would never happen. Especially now. Now that her father was dead.

Stella squirted shampoo in her hand and lathered her hair. Two months. He'd been dead two months, and she hadn't shed a tear. She stepped beneath the warm water and let it run down her head and face. She'd been at work when one of her father's lawyers had called with the news. Her mother had given out her phone number and she'd been more upset about that than about the death of her father. She'd told the lawyer she didn't care. And she didn't.

So why did she suddenly feel so alone and hollow? It was beyond ridiculous. Her father had never wanted her in his life. Had never even told Sadie about her. If Clive had lived to be a hundred and ten, he still wouldn't have wanted anything to do with Stella. So why did she suddenly feel like a piece of her was gone? Missing? Gone forever. A piece she'd never had to begin with.

Stella finished her shower and dried her hair with a towel. She stepped into a pair of white panties and wrapped a thick white hotel robe around herself. The robe felt like a nice warm embrace, and she brushed her palm across the bathroom mirror. Through the steam and smear her hand left behind, she stared at her face. She looked more like her mother than her father, but her eyes were his eyes. Blue like the Texas sky he'd lived beneath all his life.

A hairbrush lay on the counter and she grabbed it on her way out the door. Cool air flowed from open vents and brushed her bare legs as she moved from the room and down the stairs. She ran the bristles through her hair and opened the French doors to the balcony. The sultry Louisiana night wrapped her in red and gold shadows as the last few moments of the setting sun lit heavy clouds from above. Below, Bourbon Street was fired up with glowing tubes of neon and storefronts selling anything and everything from porcelain masks and Hurricanes to lap dances.

Stella sat in a wrought-iron chair as she brushed the tangles from her hair. Three floors down, tourists crowded the old city, and their laughter and chatter mixed with the streams of jazz and zydeco and the smells of food and ancient plumbing. Two balconies over, a couple shared a bottle of wine beneath the red and gold streaks in the dusky sky, the clink of their glasses and lowered voices barely audible. Stella curled her feet up beneath her and pulled her robe tight as a hotel door opened and shut. She didn't know whether it was the door to her room or not until she felt a warm tingle up her spine as a darker shadow spilled from the doorway and over her.

"Are you hungry?" he asked.

"A little." She looked over her shoulder at Beau. At his big outline lit from behind like he was a saint. All he needed was a bright red sacred heart. "Are you?"

"Kasper fed me, but I can always eat." She couldn't see his face, but she could feel his gaze. A gaze too hot, too earthy for a saint. "Give me ten minutes to shower. I know a little place a few blocks from here that serves great alligator sausage and dirty rice."

"Sounds good," Stella said, even though there was no way she was going to eat alligator. He turned to go, taking his hot, earthy gaze with him.

Stella stood and ran her fingers through her damp hair. She moved to the railing and looked down at the crowded street. She couldn't go upstairs and get dressed until Beau was finished. She supposed she could listen for the shower then run upstairs, grab some clothes, and dress downstairs. But she'd prefer just to wait until she could put on a little makeup, too. She looked at the crowded street. At friends, families, and lovers. The hollow loneliness she'd felt earlier pressed in on her heart. Why now? In one way or another, she'd always been alone. If not exactly alone, different. Her father had paid her to stay away from his family, and she'd never really fit into her mother's family. Which was probably more her fault. She'd never bothered to really learn the language and embrace the Hispanic culture. She'd been raised in it, but never really bothered to learn why a girl couldn't wear red fingernail polish. She'd just thought it was stupid. She'd had a traditional quinceañera, complete with big white dress and mariachi band, when what she'd really wanted was a sweet sixteen with a red sequined mini and Britney Spears. When she'd wanted gifts of makeup and jewelry instead of a Bible and rosary.

"Sorry about the one bedroom."

She turned and pressed her behind into the rail. He stood in the doorway wearing jeans and a dress shirt, unbuttoned and open as if it was too hot to close it. Light from inside washed over his left shoulder and down the contours of his hard chest. She bet his skin was warm and still sticky from the shower. She knew thinking like that was dangerous. Getting involved with Beau would be a mistake. One she would regret. "That was quick."

Within the shadows he shrugged, then stepped out onto the balcony. "It doesn't take long to knock the stink off."

Her nose wrinkled. "That killed the romance."

Above the noise of Bourbon Street, she heard his deep chuckle as he moved toward the rail. "You feeling all romantic, Boots?"

She folded her arms beneath her breasts and looked at him across her shoulder. More like lust than romance. "It's a romantic city."

He shoved one hip into the railing next to her, so close the open edge of his crisp shirt brushed the sleeve of her robe. "Some parts." He turned to look out at the city. "Others are very *un*romantic."

She turned toward him and gazed up into his face bathed in an eerie neon glow. "Like you."

His head snapped back toward her. "Like me?"

"Yeah. When you save damsels in distress, that's kind of romantic. But when you say stuff like knocking off your stink or pissing like a horse . . ." Again her nose wrinkled. "Not so much." His mouth was just a few inches above hers and she wondered if he would kiss her. Again. If he'd do that thing where she felt consumed, then push her away. Again. She didn't want to be pushed away. Easily set aside. Again. Getting involved with Beau might be a mistake, but she didn't care right now. Right now he was filling the hollow places with his warmth. He consumed the lonely ache in her stomach and filled it up with tingling need and curiosity. There would always be time for regret. Later.

"I usually don't save damsels in distress." Beau looked at the neon light vibrating in Stella's dark hair, and his gaze slid to the mouth and chin pointed up at him. She wore a hotel robe, and he wondered what she wore beneath. "And I've never been a romantic kind of guy." Especially now that he was on the celibacy wagon. A fact of which he had to remind himself as he looked at her mouth pointed up toward him.

"Never?"

The tip of her tongue touched the corner of her mouth and he felt it between his legs. "Maybe for an hour here and there."

"Here?"

He shook his head as the ache in his groin

prodded him to throw her over his shoulder and take her to bed. "No."

She raised her hand and placed it over his heart. Warm skin to soft palm that stole his breath and grabbed his balls in a hot grasp. "Your heart is beating fast."

"The air is thick." Which was true but not the reason his blood pounded in his veins. If anything, his heart rate should be lower at this altitude.

She untied her belt, and her voice dared him to look. "Liar."

And he did. God help him, there weren't enough MIL conversions or MOS calculations he could do in his head to keep his gaze from sliding past her throat. The material parted just enough to tease him with shadows of her plump little breast, hiding the good stuff from view. The stuff he wanted to touch and taste and feel against him. "Stella, I'm trying to do the right thing with you."

"I'm not a child." She touched his belly, and his muscles turned hard beneath her soft little hands. "I'm a grown woman, and I know the right thing for me."

The woman standing in front of him practically naked was definitely not a child, and he couldn't recall wanting a woman more than he wanted Stella. He raised his hands to the front of her robe. He grabbed the lapels and meant to shut them tight, but he couldn't. He couldn't make himself push her away this time. He would. In a minute, but first . . . He wrapped his fists in terry cloth and pulled her to the balls of her feet. Her hard nipples grazed his bare chest on the way up, and he had to lock his knees to keep from falling. Warm skin pressed into his warm skin, and her soft breasts rode his chest as he lowered his mouth to hers. Soft. She was so soft and tasted so good. Her tongue touched his and he fed her long kisses filled with hunger and longing. He wanted her. He wanted this. Standing on a balcony above Bourbon Street, he felt his hungered longing turn to burning need. The sounds of the French Quarter faded to nothing, and every nerve and cell in his body focused on her. Her wet mouth and tongue. Her warm breasts against his skin and her nipples stabbing his chest. Her hot skin sticking to his and her crotch pressed into his painful hard-on.

"Estella," he groaned, and leaned his head back. Back from the soft temptation of her lips. "You said you were hungry."

"I am." She placed her hands on the sides of his head and brought his gaze to hers. "I want to do what you talked about last night." He opened his mouth but she placed a finger over his lips. "I want to eat you up, Beau. I want to start here." She placed her hot mouth on the side of his neck. "And lick my way south."

"Jesus."

"Then you lick your way south." She slid her hands beneath his open shirt, down his sides, and curled her fingers in his waistband. "Down my stomach and belly button to the inside of my thighs. I want that, Beau. I've been thinking about it. Thinking about you."

He'd been thinking about it also. No matter how hard he tried not to think of her spread out naked in front of him, offering up his favorite snacks.

"You said it's your most important job."

He was drowning in desire and lust, and his voice came out in a dry whisper. "I also said I am on the bench."

"You can have oral sex and stay on the bench."

He knew better. She might not be a child, but she was kidding herself that oral sex wasn't sex.

"I've never had to talk a guy into getting naked," she whispered just before she took his earlobe between her teeth and bit. "I can't believe I am trying to talk you into it."

He couldn't believe it, either, and with the touch of her warm tongue, he couldn't recall why he'd ever put himself on the bench in the first place. It had something to do with saving sex until it meant something. Well, it sure as hell felt like it meant something at the moment. It meant that if he didn't have Stella he was going to explode. He took her hand in his. "Let's go."

"Where? I don't want to go out." She grabbed at

her robe with her free hand as he pulled her into the room.

"You no longer have a choice."

"What are we going to do?"

"You're getting naked." He didn't bother to shut the doors behind them. "And I'm going to eat your little hot pocket."

Chapter Ten

Skin to skin, Stella pressed further into Beau. In a whirlwind of flying pants and underwear, he'd whipped their clothes off until they knelt naked in the middle of one cleared bed.

"Stella. Stella," he whispered as his mouth slid down the side of her neck to the hollow of her throat. He was so hot to the touch, like a fever burned just beneath his skin. A fever that traveled across her skin, too. He'd wrapped one arm around her waist like a steel band, keeping her crotch pressed against the long, hard length of his burning erection. "I didn't mean for this to happen."

"Do you want to stop?" she asked, even though she was fairly certain of his answer.

His grasp tightened around her waist. "Too late."

Her head fell back and her hair brushed her bare behind. She was anxious for more and excited for what was next and completely tuned in to what he did to her. One of his big hands cupped her right breast as his thumb brushed her nipple. "Beau," she moaned, and squirmed against his penis pressed into her belly. She might be a technical virgin, but her body knew what she wanted; him between her legs. The more she squirmed, the more she wanted him. Then his wet mouth latched on to her breast and his free hand slipped between her thighs. He rolled her aching nipple beneath his tongue, and his teasing touch stroked, then slid away, leaving a wet trail to her hip and belly. He tortured her with his fingers and mouth until she grasped the sides of his head and moaned for more.

He lifted his face to hers. His gray eyes smoldered and consumed and his voice came out rough when he ordered, "Lie down, Stella." She didn't need to be told twice and he knelt between her knees. His gaze slid from her face, paused at her breasts, then continued down her stomach to her crotch. His hands skimmed down the outside of her legs to her knees. He raised them until her feet rested next to her behind. "You're beautiful, Boots."

She tried to close her legs from his scrutiny, but his palms on the insides of her thighs stopped her. His hands moved down slowly, until his thumbs parted her and touched her slick pleasure button. She sucked in a breath and he smiled. "You like that?"

She licked her dry lips and nodded.

"Have you ever been eaten up by a man who truly enjoys his work?"

She nodded, then shook her head. God, she didn't know. What did that even mean? He cupped her behind in his big hands and showed her exactly what it meant. He parted her slick flesh and kissed her there. Her back arched off the bed and he slid them both to the edge and knelt on the floor with her legs over his shoulders.

"Oh my God," she moaned as he worked her over with his hot mouth. Pleasure built inside her and sizzled as it worked its way to the surface of her skin. "Do that! Yes. There. Don't stop!"

He laughed and bit the inside of her thigh. From between her legs, he lifted his gaze. "I know what I'm doing, Stella."

Yes. Yes, he did, and he got back to doing it. He sucked her into his mouth and licked and stabbed her with his tongue, over and over until her eyes rolled back in her head. "Holy frijole y guacamole!" A searing orgasm burned through her veins, flashing across her skin from her head to the tips of her curled toes. Her back arched and she couldn't breathe. "Oh my God!" His hot mouth sucked the pleasure from her body in pulsating waves. It consumed her mind, body, and soul. She moaned something. Something that in a state of delirious euphoria might have sounded like "Beau . . . yes . . . gahh . . . I love you!" Then her brain shut down and all she could do was feel. Delicious hot pleasure that left her gasping and her heart pounding as she finally came to. She felt a soft kiss on the inside of her knee and opened her eyes.

"You okay?"

She rose to her elbows and looked down her body at him; his face was turned into her leg but his sleepy gray eyes stared back at her. *Okay?* She was probably going to be okay, but never the same. "Did I just say 'I love you'?"

"It happens."

She sat up with as much dignity as possible and slid her legs from his shoulders. "It's never happened to me."

"I got skills."

Her hair fell over her face and she pulled it to one side of her neck. "Mad skills." She slid off the bed and leaned forward to kiss his shoulder. She knelt in front of him and ran her hands over his hard arms and chest. She was eager to see if she could get him to moan and groan and lose control of his brain.

"Sit on the bed, Beau. I do my best work if my hands are free to touch you where I want."

He stood, and she buried her face in his flat stomach. She reached around and grabbed both cheeks of his hard behind. A thin line of dark blond hair circled his flat stomach and tailed lower. He was all hard muscles and tight, tan skin. He was beautiful. Like a guy in a military calendar. Mr. September. All bronze and hot and sculpted.

Her open mouth slid down his lower belly, and she slipped her palms down the backs of his legs, then up again. Touching here. Brushing there. Light touches that were meant to drive him crazy. She pulled back to look up at him. At his sleepy eyes and precise breath. He was all controlled lust and she wrapped her hand around his thick erection and slowly moved her palm up and down the hot shaft. She wondered if he ever lost control. Went crazy. She ran her tongue up his engorged penis and licked the sticky bead of moisture from the cleft. His eyes got a little darker. A little more stormy, and she asked, "Ready?"

He locked his fingers behind his head and spread his feet shoulder-width apart. "Do your worst."

She smiled and ran her tongue up and down the length of him. She had a few mad skills of her own. Some she'd learned, others she read about in *Cosmo* and *Redbook* and was curious to try. She used the underside of her tongue on the sweet spot just below the head. He sucked in a breath and she sucked him into her mouth. She looked up at him watching her. She used her hands and tongue and mouth to drag a tortured groan from deep in his throat. The more she worked him over, the more she liked it. The more she liked it, the more she wanted more. His hands fell to the side of her head and he tangled his fingers in her hair. He said something about how good it felt, but he didn't lose control. Not even when she used her tongue tornado on him. He groaned and told her not to stop, but he didn't lose it. Not like her. Not even when she cupped his testicles in her hand and sucked an orgasm from him that sounded like it came from deep down in his soul. His muscles turned hard and he swore like a Marine, but he didn't lose control. Not even when she stayed with him to the end. When his muscles relaxed and he let out his breath. Not even when she stood and slid up his body, his still erect penis between them.

"You okay?" she asked as she wrapped her arms around his neck.

"You're good at that, Boots."

She smiled. "I got mad skills, too."

He kissed her forehead. "Ready for some room service?"

Her brow wrinkled and she pressed herself against his erection. "You want food?"

"Not for me. You're going to be up all night and need your strength."

She laughed. "What if I'm tired?" She totally wasn't.

"If you wanted sleep, you shouldn't have woken the beast."

● ● ●

The beast.

Stella bit the inside of her cheek and turned her face to look out the passenger window of the SUV. She gazed at the tall skinny pines of central Louisiana as memories of the previous night's experience with *the beast* flashed in her head.

After the first encounter, Beau had ordered gumbo and jambalaya and pecan pie from a restaurant in the Quarter. It had arrived with a white Sancerre, and they'd gorged on rich Cajun food and French wine. Then they'd gorged on each other, finally falling asleep in the wee hours of the morning.

Memories of his warm hands and hot mouth and slick tongue licking wine from her breasts and belly made her smile, but the memory of things he'd learned in a Hong Kong massage parlor set her cheeks on fire. Things that gave new meaning to "happy ending."

She felt his gaze on her from across the SUV and turned to look at him. He was once again clean-cut Captain American. The late morning sun lit up his hair and white T-shirt like he was a superhero. Not the talented badass who knew things. Things she'd never even read about. Things that made her say "I love you" when she clearly didn't.

"What?" he asked.

"What?"

"Your face is getting red."

"It's hot outside," she said, which was an obvious lie since they were in a vehicle with the air-conditioning blasting. She took a sip of her second latte of the day and brought up the embarrassing moment before he did. "Sorry about the 'I love you' last night."

He shrugged, and an arrogant smile twisted the corners of his lips. "Like I said, it happens."

"Well, it's never happened to me before. Has it ever happened to you?" she asked, although she figured she knew the answer.

"What? Screaming 'I love you' at the height of orgasm?" He shook his head. "Nah. I told you I'm not romantic."

Yep, that's what she'd figured. "I don't think I screamed." He was too restrained, even at the height of ecstasy.

"You screamed."

She hid her smile behind her cup. "Maybe I raised my voice a little. I couldn't help it once I beheld *the beast.*"

He laughed. A sexy, masculine chuckle that worked its way out. "You must be growing on me. That was actually funny."

"Thank you."

"You're welcome, Boots."

Now a question she'd been wondering about since Biloxi. "Are you really 'on the bench'?"

He turned his gaze to the road. "Obviously not now."

"Because of last night?"

"Yeah. I know you're going to say that what we did last night wasn't sex. You can believe that if you want. I'm not judging you, but I know better."

They hadn't had sex. They'd fooled around. There was a difference but she wasn't going to split hairs and argue with him. Not when her body still tingled with afterglow. "Why are you, or were you, on the bench? You're obviously not a virgin so that bird has flown the coop. You're an attractive, healthy man and—" She gasped. "Is there something wrong with you?"

"No, but if you are concerned about that," he said as a frown settled across his brow, "don't you think you should have asked before now?"

Yes! But he was Beau. Captain America, and she felt so safe and protected around him.

"Don't you think you should have asked last night?" He glanced at her, then back at the road. "For the record, I'm clean as a monk."

"Me too."

"I know."

"How?" He was so annoying. "Are you a super secret spy *and* undercover gynecologist?"

"My face was closer to your muffin than your gynecologist." Again he glanced at her. "I would have noticed."

"You checked me out?"

"Of course. A guy can't be too careful what he puts in his mouth."

He was right. He wasn't romantic and it was time to turn this verbal train around. "Did a woman break your heart? Is that why you're on the bench?"

"No."

That was it? Just a no? What would make a man swear off women? A good-looking man like Sergeant Beau Junger. "Are you having a mid-life crisis?"

"No." He frowned and reached for a bottle of water in the cup holder. He steered the SUV with one forearm as he unscrewed the cap. "I have a few more years before I hit *mid-life*."

She thought of her old boyfriend who'd stolen her Banana Republic coat. "Are you having a bisexual crisis?"

He choked a little on his water. "What?" He looked at her and wiped a few drops from his chin. "No. I'm not having any sort of crisis, Jesus." He turned his attention to the road and shoved the bottle back into the holder. This time he added, "Can't a man sit on the bench for a while without having a crisis? Can't I just want sex to mean something with a woman I care about *first,* for a fucking change?"

"Oh." She felt a stab in her chest, and she sharply turned her face away. "Oh wow."

"Shit. That came out wrong."

She didn't think so, and she didn't know which hurt worse. That he didn't care about her or that what they'd done last night meant nothing. Not that it did mean anything. Or must. Or . . . or should. But somehow it felt like it did. At least for her. "Sorry I forced you to fool around."

"You're not big enough to force me into doing anything." In a surprising move, he reached across the SUV and took her hand in his. The heat from his palm tingled the inside of her wrist and elbow. "I didn't do anything last night I haven't been thinking about doing since I first saw you in those little leather shorts last week."

She glanced across her shoulder at him and tried not to let his simple touch affect her and make her think of where he'd touched her last night. "I thought you didn't like me when we first met."

"I thought you were annoying. I didn't know you well enough to dislike you." He gave her hand a squeeze. "I liked your tight ass in those shorts, though. Tried not to stare at it when we were leaving Ricky's parking lot."

"You stared at my behind while I was freaked out about Ricky?"

"Sure."

"Even though I annoyed you?"

"Of course. One doesn't have anything to do with the other."

Yes it did. That was just stupid. She couldn't

imagine looking at a man she found super annoying and seeing anything attractive about any part of . . . Wait. Yes she could. She was looking at him now.

"You're beautiful, Stella Leon, and I broke my own rules with you."

"Rules? There's more than one?"

He let go of her hand and held up one finger. "Don't have sex until you're married or at least headed in that direction." He held up another finger. "Never get involved with a buddy's sister, wife, or girlfriend." And one last. "Don't mix business and pleasure. I broke all three with you."

"I'm not a buddy's sister, wife, or girlfriend," she pointed out.

"When Vince marries Sadie, you'll be his sister."

Technically, she supposed. "So, should I be sorry I 'woke the beast'?"

"Are you?"

"Are you?"

He glanced at her. "No."

She tried not to smile and failed. "No.

"So, I'm business *and* pleasure?" She put her empty cup in the holder next to his. "Am I busin-sure?" She kind of liked that. "Or pleas-ness?" She liked that better. More romantic.

He glanced at her. "Boots, you're head goat in a classic goat rodeo."

She gasped and pointed at herself. "I'm a goat?"

"You're the head goat." He laughed like that

was funny. "A cute head goat. How is that?"

"I don't want to be a goat at all." Her cousin had raised goats. They butted people with their horns and pooped a lot. They weren't all that cute. "What kind of goat are you?"

"I'm the goat herder."

She opened her mouth to argue but his phone rang and ended the conversation. He didn't say hello, just hit talk and said, "Hey maggot." Then he laughed. Stella supposed that if it came down to it, she'd rather be a cute goat than a maggot.

"About two hours from the Texas state line," Beau continued.

Two hours. Two hours closer to meeting Sadie. Stella dug around in her backpack and pulled out her red lipstick. She put it on for something to do with her hands.

"No. From Dallas it's about another six. I'll shave it to five."

Five hours. They'd talked about stopping for the night in Dallas before continuing to the panhandle the next morning. For a few hours she'd forgotten why she was sitting in an Escalade speeding toward Lovett, Texas.

"I'm still on the road, so call the office and leave the intel with Deb."

About this time tomorrow, she'd be at the JH, her father's ranch. Now her sister's ranch. The one place on the planet where she'd always known she was not welcome.

Two hours closer to the Texas state line. She didn't know whether to be afraid or excited. She was probably both. She drummed her fingers on the middle console and took a deep breath. Either way, her stomach felt all light and queasy like she was going to vomit.

Beau hung up his phone and tossed it on the dash. "Everything that was in your apartment is now in a storage unit in northeast Miami."

"Oh."

Beau glanced at the back of Stella's head as she turned and stared out the passenger side window. Strands of her dark hair fell across her shoulder and down her bare arm. Last night he'd held her soft hair in his hands as she'd used her softer mouth on him. He didn't know if it was because he hadn't had sexual contact in eight months, or her, but he couldn't remember anything that good.

"I guess my car will be okay for a few days until I can get it."

His gaze dropped to her breasts in a little blue dress before he looked back at the road. Best not to think about her breasts. Not too small. Not too big. Perfectly fit in his hands. Jesus. "Miami is still too hot. The Gallo brothers showed up and tried to intimidate my guys." He would have loved to have witnessed the two mobsters trying to muscle three Marines.

"They haven't given up?"

"I guess Lou Gallo is real bitter about his hand," he joked.

She looked over at him with big blue eyes and full red lips. "Did they learn where I am?"

They were actually more interested in him. "Nah, but they did learn not to mess with pumped-up Marines with serious attitude problems."

Her eyes got big and looked like they were getting a little watery. "Don't worry." He surprised himself again by reaching for her hand. He usually wasn't *that* guy. In fact, he'd never been the type of guy to pat a woman on the back or shoulder or take her hand like they were friends or something awkward like that. Only with Stella it didn't feel awkward. More like a chance to touch her. A chance to touch her that he should avoid but couldn't. "They won't find you."

She swallowed hard and reminded him of the other day when he'd found her hiding outside the airport. Young. Scared. Vulnerable. So sexy he wanted to do real bad things to her. Some of which he'd done the night before. Her red mouth, soft and slick on his—

"Pull over. I'm going to be sick!"

"What?"

She rolled down the window and fanned her face. "I'm going to be sick!"

Beau didn't have to be told more than twice. He jerked the steering wheel to the left and exited the interstate. The SUV skidded to a halt in the middle of a flat grassy field, and the passenger door flew open and Stella jumped out. A rusted-out red-and-white Ford rattled down the exit as Beau got out of the Cadillac. He grabbed a bottle of water and walked around the front. Stella stood with her hands on her bare knees, her hair falling forward like a shiny black curtain.

"Do you need some water?" he asked as he moved toward her.

She nodded and gasped for breath.

"Breathe, Boots."

"I'm scared."

"You're going to pass out."

She pulled air deep into her lungs and let it out.

"Are you going to puke?"

She straightened and pushed her hair from her pale face. "No. I'm having a panic attack, though."

"Ricky and his boys will never find you." He unscrewed the plastic bottle cap and handed her the water.

"I don't want to go to Texas." She took a drink and it dribbled down her chin.

Texas?

"I can't go." She took another small drink and wiped her chin with the back of her hand. "What if she doesn't like me?"

Stella wasn't making sense. "Who?"

"Sadie."

"Sadie?" He moved to stand in front of her and

looked deep into her blue eyes. They were still wide and a little out of focus. "This is about Sadie?"

She nodded and took another deep breath.

"Why wouldn't she like you?"

"I annoy people sometimes," she said on a big exhale. "I annoyed you."

"That's just because I wanted to touch your butt and couldn't."

"Seriously?" She licked her red lips and took a drink. "Are you just saying that to be nice?"

"No, I'm not just trying to be nice. And yes, you have a seriously nice butt." He gave her a reassuring smile and said, "Tell me about Texas."

A white minivan drove past on the exit while vehicles on the interstate filled the air with tire noise. She raised her free hand to her bare throat and confessed, "I'm afraid to go to Texas, and I didn't tell you because you're not afraid of anything."

She was wrong. He was looking at his biggest fear. Into the blue eyes and pretty face of a temptation so strong he'd given in rather than fight it. He'd broken the rules with her. Behaved less than honorably. "You're one of the strongest women I know." He'd never broken his own rules, at least not three at the same time.

"I'm not." Her hand slid down her tan throat to just above her heart and Beau's gaze followed.

"What if I get there and Sadie can see I'm not good enough?"

His gaze flew to hers. "Not good enough? She doesn't even know you."

She closed her eyes tight and clenched her hand over her heart. "That came out wrong. I mean . . . I mean . . ." She opened her eyes and looked at him. "Our father didn't like me. He never wanted to have anything to do with me. What if I meet her and she's like him? What if she's like Clive? What if she takes one look at me and doesn't want to know me?"

"She wants to see you." He cupped her cheeks in his palms. "She sent me to find you. Remember?"

She swallowed hard. "One time my father came to New Mexico. I thought he wanted to see me. I thought . . . I don't know. That he cared about me. He brought me porcelain horses and cowboy boots. I think I was ten or eleven. I don't know. He stayed for about an hour and I was so happy. So—happy." Her voice broke but she didn't cry. "I thought he finally cared about me." She shook her head. "That's so pathetic. Worse, I even remember what he was wearing. I remember how tall he looked when he walked out the door, and I remember that I waved but he didn't look back. Watching him leave broke my heart. I didn't know it would be the last time I ever saw him."

Beau had no idea what to say. He had no idea

what to do to take the pain out of Stella's eyes. Anger worked its way up his spine. He felt like a kid again when he'd find his mother crying in her bed or on the floor in the closet. He felt helpless.

"Then I found out he didn't come that day to see me because he cared or even liked me. He came because he was at a horse auction in the area and he felt obliged to stop by. He just happened to be in Las Cruces and felt an obligation to check in with my mother. Just a meaningless obligation, like the trust fund."

Beau knew how to survive in the desert or at the North Pole. He knew what to do if he was stranded in the middle of the ocean or pinned down by insurgents. With Stella, he was totally out of his element and had been since the night he'd walked into Ricky's and seen her in little leather shorts and Amy Winehouse wig.

"What if Sadie just feels an obligation like Clive? What if she walks back out of my life just as easily as her father?"

Beau slid his hands through her hair to the back of her head and tilted her pretty face up to him. He'd broken his rules with her. Since the day she'd run to him with her backpack and duffel, the lines had blurred. The mission got fuzzy. "I won't let that happen."

"How?"

He didn't know, and instead of answering, he

lowered his mouth and kissed her. On the side of the interstate in northeast Louisiana. Where rules and honor got fuzzy and nothing made sense. Nothing but her red lips pressed to his.

Chapter Eleven

Stella stood in the dirt driveway of a white clapboard house and stared at the big double doors with an H burned into the wood like it had been branded. Dogs barked somewhere in the distance, and the bright setting sun cast her shadow onto the edge of the lawn and stone sidewalk.

Her father's house. Her sister's house. The house where she'd been conceived but never been welcome. Her fingers tingled and she shook her hands.

Beau's reassuring palm found the small of her back and his shadow joined hers. "Breathe, Boots."

"I can't."

"Sure you can." His thumb brushed her skin through her new paisley dress and sent a tingle up her spine. "You've faced more difficult situations."

"Like?"

"Ricky. Fat Fabian and Lefty Lou."

That seemed like an eternity ago. She licked

her dry lips and swallowed. "Do I look okay?" They'd been driving six hours and she'd done her best to look good, but her hands had shaken badly when she'd tried to freshen up her makeup on the road between Lovett and the JH.

"You look beautiful, Stella."

She probably looked more like a scared chicken. She certainly felt like one. Although she didn't know if chickens got scared. Maybe she was mixing them up with cats. She didn't know. Her brain was numb. Her chest felt tight. She couldn't breathe. "I'm nervous."

"I know, but I'm here. I've got your six."

She looked up into the reflection of herself in his sunglasses. She didn't know if she looked like a chicken or a cat, but she did look scared shitless. "What's that?"

"Your back. If you want to leave now, we'll leave. It's not too late." He pointed over his shoulder at the black Escalade. "If you want to leave in ten minutes, I'll get you out of here."

In a few short days, he'd become her anchor. Her rock. The calm strength by her side. And in a few short days, he'd be gone. The thought of it made her feel even more panicky. "With flash-bang?"

"If that's what you want. We'll light it up. Just say the word."

One side of the big doors opened and a more pressing panic pushed the thought of Beau to the back of her mind. A tall blonde stood in the shadows of the doorway and Stella whispered, "Sadie." Or maybe she'd just whispered it in her own head. A tall man appeared in the doorway behind Sadie and put his hands on her shoulders.

"That's Vince," Beau told her, and pushed Stella ahead a few steps. "He's a good guy."

Stella's feet felt heavy as she put one foot in front of the other and tried to take it all in. The big house. Her sister watching her. Beau's hand on her back. Her heart pounding in her throat. It was too much. Too much, and she stopped in the middle of the sidewalk. Everything slowed, then stood still. As still as Stella. One second. Two. Three. Everything seemed frozen, then she blinked and her sister was moving toward her. Fast.

"Estella Immaculata Leon-Hollowell?"

Sadie stopped in front of her. Close enough to touch. For the first time in twenty-eight years. "Yes." She waited. Her breath tight in her lungs.

Sadie's eyes stared down into hers. Looking for something. Looking. "Lord, your name is a mouthful."

"Everyone calls me Stella."

Looking into her soul. Waiting. "You have Daddy's eyes."

She swallowed. Sadie was stunning. Like her mother, the Texas beauty queen. She was at least six inches taller than Stella and thin like their father.

"I didn't know if you'd come."

"I did," she stated the obvious and instantly felt stupid. Sadie went to college. She was smart. She—

"I'm so glad." Sadie put her hand on the peach-colored blouse covering her stomach and smiled. "I've been nervous as a long-tailed cat."

"I told you Beau would get her here."

Stella raised her gaze to the big man sliding his arm around Sadie's waist. He had dark hair and green eyes and shoulders as big as Beau's.

"I'm Vince Haven." He held out his hand toward Stella. "Sadie has been pacing for days. I'm glad you're finally here and she can relax."

Stella shook his hand and her chest didn't feel quite so tight. Sadie had been nervous, too. "It's a pleasure, Vince."

Vince raised his gaze to the man by her side. "Beau. It's good to see you."

The two men shook hands and Stella felt the loss of Beau's touch against her back. "How the hell are you, Haven?"

"Good." He introduced his fiancée to Beau and Sadie's eyes rounded.

"There *are* two of you," she said. "Lord have mercy."

"I'm the good twin." Beau chuckled. "Is Blake around?"

Vince shook his head. "He's out raising hell someplace. He's been staying at my apartment, and I'm afraid to go over there."

The two men exchanged looks filled with hidden meaning and Sadie motioned for Stella to follow her. "Let's go inside while these two catch up and talk about the good old days when they slept in swamps and ate bugs."

Stella glanced back at Beau. "You ate bugs?"

He grinned. "One or two."

She followed Sadie, and her gaze lowered to her sister's khaki skirt, long legs, and cowboy boots. They moved through the big double doors and into her father's house. A chandelier made out of antlers hung in the entry, and worn Navaho rugs covered the wood floors. She looked back, through the door and across the yard. Beau laughed at something Vince said, but his gaze was on her. Touching her across the distance and reminding her of the other places he'd touched her last night. Teaching her things she didn't know about. Things that stopped just short of penetration and made her lose control. Something she noticed that never happened to him. Not like it happened to her.

"I could use some wine," Sadie said, and shut the door behind them. "How about you?"

Stella clenched her hands, then relaxed them to let some of the tension out. "That sounds great. Thank you."

"We'll sit in the parlor. Don't let the couch scare you." Sadie pointed to a room across the entry. "I'll be right back."

Stella's jeweled flip-flops slapped her heels as she walked into the parlor. Another big chandelier of antlers lit the room dominated by cowhide furniture and an enormous rock fireplace. A portrait of a horse hung above the mantel and family pictures sat around the room in heavy frames. The room smelled of lemon oil and leather, and Stella reached for the picture on an end table.

Clive Hollowell with a young Sadie on his shoulders. He looked like Stella remembered. Hard and lean and intimidating as heck. A big smile lit Sadie's young eyes while Clive looked stone-faced.

"That's my favorite photo," Sadie said as she walked into the room. "Daddy is almost smiling."

Stella set the photo back down and turned. "Thank you," she said, and took a glass of white wine from her sister.

"I have a million things to ask you. A million things to say." Sadie's gaze moved across Stella's face as if trying to take in everything at once. "But I can't think of one right now."

Stella felt the same and sat next to Sadie on the couch. "I never thought I'd be here. Just never thought . . ." She lifted her free hand and let it fall to her lap. "That I'd meet you."

"Have you always known of me?" Sadie took a sip, her attention locked on Stella as if she couldn't look away.

Stella nodded. She couldn't look away, either. From the sister she'd seen only in old news clippings. "My mother told me about you. She was your nanny."

"I remember Marisol. My mama had just died and Daddy couldn't abide my crying." Finally Sadie looked down at the hem of her skirt and smoothed it with her fingers. "So he hired your mama to look after me. I was only five, but I remember she was nice to me and brushed my hair every day. After she left, my hair was usually a mess unless Clara Anne, our housekeeper, fixed if for me."

That was one thing she could say about her mother. Stella might not have had the most expensive or designer labels, but she'd always been clean and polished. "My mother braided my hair every morning until I was about seven. I hated it."

"I think I would have liked that." Sadie looked up. "But isn't it the way of things. We think we want what we never had."

What did she mean? Was it a warning not to want too much? "I don't want anything from you."

"Lord, I never thought you did. If you'd wanted anything from me, I wouldn't have had to find a big Marine to track you down." Sadie took a drink and set her glass on the table. "Knowing Blake as I do, I was afraid his brother might scare you off."

Stella smiled and took a sip of wine. It wet her dry throat and she said, "He looks kind of scary, but I wasn't afraid of him." Oddly.

"Vince told me there was a problem at the bar where you work."

"Worked." Her gaze slid away to an antler lamp. "I kind of quit, but I'll get a new job. Good bartenders can always find work and I make good tips." She didn't want to sound like too big a loser so she added, "I'll probably work part-time while I go to school." She stood because she was too restless to sit while she boldly lied. "Beautiful horse," she said, and pointed to the portrait above the fireplace.

"That's Admiral. He was Daddy's Blue Roan Tovero. The day Admiral died was the only time I'd ever seen Daddy close to tears." She moved and stood next to Stella. "Daddy cared for horses more than he did people."

Stella looked up at her sister. Her sister. She still couldn't believe she stood in her father's house looking at his Blue Roan Tovero. Stella actually did know a thing or two about paint horses. She'd written a paper on them in high school because she'd thought they were pretty. "I feel weird being here. Clive never wanted me here."

"My daddy . . . our father was a difficult man." Sadie turned her attention to the painting. "I never understood him. I spent a lot of time trying. I spent a lot of time trying to please him, too. I never did."

"But he *loved* you." The implication hung in the air, sounding a lot like Stella cared, and she didn't.

"In his way, I guess." Sadie shrugged a shoulder and turned to look at Stella. "But if he really loved me, why didn't he tell me I had a little sister? I had a right to know. I had a right to know you." Her eyes got a little watery. "I would have reached out to you, Stella. I would have made sure you were in my life."

"That's probably why he never told you." Stella drained her wine. Did she really feel a little bit sorry for Sadie? Her sister who had everything? Not that she cared about things and possessions, but at least their father had loved her. Even if it was in *his own way*. "He never wanted me in his life."

"That's just mean. I always knew he could be cold, but that's just cruel." Anger tightened her lips. "How could he abandon a child?"

"He made sure my mother had money to raise me." Was she really defending Clive?

"Well, I should hope to shout. That was the very least he could do." She turned her attention back to the horse painting. "A few days before he died, I thought we'd gotten closer. We didn't fall on each other's necks, and there was no touching Hollywood moment, but I thought we were finally relating on some adult level." She laughed without humor. "He told me he'd never liked cattle and always wanted to be a truck driver."

Stella couldn't imagine the tall, thin man she knew driving the big rigs.

"Like telling me that he's always wanted to be a trucker was more important than telling me I have a sister. He was sick. He knew he was dying. He was almost eighty, and still he couldn't tell me? He couldn't say, 'I always hated cattle and wanted to be a king of the road.'" Sadie paused to hold up one finger. "'Oh, and by the way, Sadie Jo, you have a sister'? I had to discover it on my own when I read his will?" She looked at Stella and again placed a hand on her stomach. "Here I am, getting angry all over again while you have a right to be more angry than anyone." She took in a deep breath, and the light from the antler chandelier shone in her hair. "More wine?"

"Is the pope Catholic?"

Sadie smiled. "Lord, I hope so. If not, he's just some old person with a preference for weird hats, like my dead Aunt Ginger."

Stella laughed. "My uncle Jorge has a sombrero with shot glasses hanging on it like tassel fringe. Some are chipped and broken, but he wears it every Cinco de Mayo. It's lovely."

"I could use a shot of Patron." Sadie glanced at

Stella out of the corners of her eyes as they moved down a hall past a fancy dining room with heavy drapery. "Maybe two, but I don't want you to think I'm a big drinker."

"Then I'll pour."

Vince Haven had always had an affinity for the Marine Corps. The blood and guts sledge hammers at the point of the spear. Usually the first infantry units to arrive and deliver the big thump. They were tough and mean and convinced of their own superiority. Vince liked that about Marines, even though everyone knew Navy SEALs were the elite within the special operations community. He'd hate to have to physically prove that point to Sergeant Junger, though. He'd cleared a few bars with the Junger boys, then watched in complete bafflement as they turned on each other. Knocking the snot out of each other until they both lay on the ground. Too winded to move, but still arguing over who was tougher, Batman or Superman.

"How long will you be in town?" Vince asked as he leaned his hip into the black Escalade. He noticed Beau check his watch for about the twentieth time in the past half hour.

"I'll stick around for a few days." The Marine glanced at the front doors of the JH. "Depends on Blake."

Blake? Vince wondered if his brother was the

only person Beau was sticking around for, or perhaps a little brunette with red lips? "Did Stella tell you her plans?" Blake had mentioned the fiasco at Stella's work, and Beau had filled in the rest.

"I don't know that she's a planner." He pushed his sunglasses to the top of his head and it was scary how much he looked like his brother. Vince had spent enough time with Blake, in the teams and after, to detect the slight differences in the shape of their jaws and eyes. And of course, Blake had a scar on his chin. "As far as I can tell, she's more like a dandelion seed. She goes where the wind blows her and takes root."

"That's what concerns me." When Sadie had first learned of Stella, she'd been hurt and confused. He hated to see that kind of pain in her eyes. "A flighty dandelion seed."

"I wouldn't call her flighty. She's too responsible to be flighty." He shook his head as he reached inside his side pants pocket and pulled out his cell phone. "More impulsive."

Impulsive? "How well did you get to know her?"

"I've spent the last six days with her, most of the time in an Escalade." He pushed a few buttons on his phone and frowned. "An Escalade is big, but isn't that big. What exactly do you want to know, Vince?"

A few things. He'd noticed Beau's hand in the

small of Stella's back as they'd walked toward the house. There were certain places a man rested his hand when he was real comfortable with a woman. When she belonged to him. He wondered if Beau was still riding the no-sex wagon or if he'd jumped off onto Sadie's little sister. "Sadie was real hurt and upset that her father never told her she had a sister." He decided not to ask about the past six days and nights. At least not right now. "I guess I just don't want Stella to hurt her, too."

"Copy that, but it's more likely Stella is the one who gets hurt," he said, an edge to his voice as he punched out a quick text. "I'd really hate to see that." He shoved the phone back in his pants pocket. "She's been through enough rejection from the Hollowells."

Vince looked into Beau's steel-gray eyes. The guy gave nothing away. Real cool. "Sadie isn't going to reject Stella. More likely she's going to buy one of those 'I'm a Big Sister' T-shirts and matching heart necklaces." And it was his job to protect her from an unknown sister who might see an opportunity to take advantage of Sadie's optimism and hope. It was his job to grill the girl to make sure she wanted a relationship with her sister and not something else. "The town is going to go crazy, though."

"How's that?"

Beau was the kind of cool that came with years of surviving in the pressure cooker of war.

"Nothing much happens in Lovett. So when the town hears that Clive Hollowell has a twenty-eight-year-old illegitimate daughter, they're going to kill to get eyes on her." His aunt Luraleen would likely lead the scouting party.

Beau checked his watch again. "I'm meeting Blake at someplace called the Road Kill Bar."

Vince laughed. "Don't wreck the place."

Beau finally smiled and walked to the back of the SUV. "I don't drink like that anymore." He opened the doors and pulled out a backpack and duffel. "It takes me too long to recover these days."

"Roger that." Vince didn't drink much these days. Not like Blake. Blake drank like he was on leave and Vince wondered if he should alert Beau before he walked into the Road Kill. "Are those Stella's?" He'd find out soon enough.

"Yeah."

"Go meet your brother. I'll take those."

Beau hesitated before he gave them over. "Tell Stella to give me a shout if she needs anything."

"Will do." He shook Beau's free hand, then took the duffel and backpack. "Stay at my place with Blake and have him bring you by the Gas and Go tomorrow," he said, referring to the convenience store he'd spent the past few months renovating. He turned toward the house and waved a parting hand. For the last eight weeks or so, he'd lived at the JH with Sadie. It seemed natural and right and better than he'd ever thought possible.

Unfortunately, it also gave the town something to gossip about besides the Hendersons' mysterious septic tank explosion. His moving into the JH had even eclipsed the scandalous discovery that the newest deputy had shacked up with Lily Darlington. Stella's arrival would give the town something new to feast on. Hollowell gossip was the juiciest kind, and he went in search of the long-lost sisters.

He found them in the kitchen. Giggling. The bags in his hands hit the floor as he watched his fiancée down a straight shot. "You're drinking?" He looked at the bottle on the counter. "Tequila?" Sadie never drank tequila. It made her wild and crazy. The last time she'd had one too many margaritas she'd sung "I'm Too Sexy" at Slim Clem's karaoke night, then passed out on the pool table.

Sadie smiled. "It's okay, Vince. Stella is a professional."

He turned to the petite woman squeezing lemons into a martini shaker. Lord, she was small. "Professional what?"

"Mixologist," Stella provided, her big eyes all innocent as she added a bit of sugar. "It's one of the more highly skilled and sought-after careers in the industry. It takes a quick mind, steady hand, and knife skills."

What industry?

Sadie nodded like she knew what the hell her sister was talking about. "Like all impalement arts."

"Exactly. It's like sword swallowing or knife throwing." She put the lid on the shaker. "Or open heart surgery."

Sadie laughed like her sister was just hilarious. Vince didn't get the joke, but that was okay. Sadie's laughter was more than enough. He moved toward the woman he loved and cupped her face in his palms. "You good?"

She nodded. "Thanks, Vin." She kissed the side of his hand. "I owe you."

"Hooyah."

"Maybe two hooyahs."

He chuckled and dropped his hands.

"Are we ready for round two?" Stella asked as she poured from the shaker into three tall shot glasses.

Vince preferred a cold beer, but what the hell.

Stella passed out the glasses.

"What is this?"

"A lemon margarita shot, minus the infused vanilla."

"*La familia,*" Sadie said as she held up her shot.

Stella raised her glass. "To family."

"Family." Vince took his shot. It was a little sweet and girly for his liking.

Sadie's lips puckered.

Stella blew out a breath and smiled. "Where's Beau?"

Vince would stick with a cold Lone Star. "He left to meet Blake at the Road Kill."

"Oh." Her smile fell and she looked behind Vince as if Beau was hiding behind him. "Is he coming back tonight?"

Beau might be one cool hard-to-read dude, but Stella was an open book. "He said to give him a call if you need anything."

"Oh." She turned and put her shot glass on the counter, but not before Vince noticed the confusion pulling at her forehead. "So, I guess that means he won't be back tonight."

Vince shot a glance at Sadie, who lifted a brow in response. "I'll take your bags upstairs," he volunteered.

She looked so young as she glanced from Sadie to Vince, then back again. "I guess I'm staying here?"

"Of course!" Sadie moved toward her sister and put her hand on Stella's shoulder. "Where would you stay if not here?"

"Well, I thought I'd stay in a motel."

"Why? Why would you even think about staying in a motel?"

"Well, what if you saw me and didn't like me? Or . . . or I didn't like you?" She shrugged. "It's weird being here."

Vince felt bad. Bad that she didn't feel comfortable in her father's house. Bad that she hadn't been sure if her sister would like her.

"I'll take your stuff," he said, and reached for her bags. Yeah, he felt bad, but he was still going to grill the girl like a cheese sandwich.

Chapter Twelve

Beau woke to the sound of someone puking his guts up. *Blake*. Beau bunched the pillow beneath his head and looked up at the ceiling fan over his head. Vince's apartment was your typical two-bedroom, two-bath space. The complex was new and still smelled of new carpet.

The water in the bathroom down the hall turned on, and Beau sat up and swung his legs over the side of the bed. He'd have preferred to wake up in a hotel room with Stella curled up by his side. Like the last two mornings. Her warm, soft bottom pressed into his hard dick and one of his hands cupping her breast. Was it just yesterday he'd woken and kissed her bare shoulder? Twenty-four hours ago that she'd arched against him and moaned. That he'd taken that as an invitation to slide his erection between her thighs, high against her slick crotch, and to teach her how to ride him until she came. She hadn't shouted that she loved him. Not like the first time, and he was relieved.

Stella didn't love him any more than he loved

her. Love took time. More time than six days in a SUV and two nights of sex. Good sex. Sex without penetration. Creative sex that challenged his abilities and control, but Beau had always thrived on challenges.

He rose from the bed and entered the master bathroom. With the head of his penis pressed into the apex of her hot, wet thighs, it would have been so easy to make her want it all. To make her want him so bad that she wanted him deep inside, all the way. Feel her wet and tight around him. Make it so good she wouldn't care. Make her so hot she'd want it again.

It would have been so easy, but even as hot, consuming lust had chewed him up inside and out, he hadn't given in to it. He wouldn't exactly call his control admirable. No, admirable would have been if he'd had the willpower to walk away from her in New Orleans, but he hadn't walked away. He'd taken what she'd offered. He wasn't sorry, but neither would he dishonor Stella or himself by talking her out of her virginity. She wanted to save that final act for a man she loved and wanted to live with for the rest of her life.

A man that wasn't he.

Several times throughout the previous night, he'd thought of stepping outside the bar and giving her a call. He hadn't because his job was done. His responsibility over. Free from his continual presence and the confines of the

Escalade, he was sure she felt the same. They'd had a good time for a few days, but it was over.

He took a shower and brushed his teeth and wondered what kind of shape his brother would be in this morning. Considering that he'd had to help his brother into the apartment, he'd guess somewhere between shitty and wanting to shoot himself. God knew Beau wanted to shoot him.

The Road Kill was a typical cowboy bar complete with dance floor, stuffed animals, and long horns mounted on the walls. For a Tuesday night, the bar had been fairly busy, but Beau had recognized his brother's laugh the moment he'd entered the building. Blake sat at a table surrounded by men in trucker hats and women with big hair.

It was always good to see Blake, but he would have preferred not to spend the night in a crowded bar while his brother drank among strangers.

Blake was part of him in a way that people without a twin couldn't comprehend. They walked, talked, and chewed their food the same. They looked the same and thought the same because they were one and the same. He knew Blake like he knew himself. He saw himself when he looked at his brother, yet they were their own men. Perhaps more alike than different, but different in many ways.

Beau liked green beans. Blake, peas. Beau listened to hard rock. Blake preferred country. In his free time, Beau liked to kick back and catch a ball game. Blake liked to kick back in bars and hold court.

Like their dad.

Beau dressed in cargo pants and a black T-shirt and wasn't surprised to see his brother standing in the kitchen wearing the same thing. They had the same taste and it happened more often than not. He was more surprised to see Blake's waistline in the light of day. His brother wasn't fat. Far from it, but he was definitely on the way to getting a beer gut.

"How you feeling?" Beau asked as he opened a cupboard looking for a coffee mug.

"My head's pounding like a bitch." Blake opened a cabinet and pulled out a bright pink "crazy cowgirl" mug. "Nothing a few Advil and coffee won't cure." He poured and handed the coffee to Beau.

Beau noticed his brother's cup had a SEALs trident on it. "This yours?" He held up the pink mug, then took a drink.

Blake laughed. "I imagine it's Sadie's, but I thought it matched your personality, sissy ass jarhead."

"More like it matches the color of your eyeballs, squid shit."

Blake opened the refrigerator and pulled out a half gallon of milk. "Did you meet Sadie?" Subject of bloodshot eyes closed.

Beau didn't want to talk about his brother's drinking anyway. He was in town for only a short time, and fighting with Blake wasn't high on his list of entertainment. "Briefly."

"She's a nice lady." He added a splash of milk to his coffee, then handed it to Beau. "Vince is a lucky guy."

"He seems happy." He stirred the milk into his coffee. "He said something about stopping by the store you two have been renovating."

"The Gas and Go. It's not far from here." He shoved his hand into his pocket and pulled out his keys. "Let's grab some breakfast at the Wild Coyote first."

"I'll drive," Beau said as he pulled out his own keys. "Your truck is parked at the bar."

The Wild Coyote advertised their "World Famous Breakfast Casserole" on the front of the diner and on the menus. Beau didn't know what made it "World Famous," but he took one look at the photo inside the menu and ordered the Coyote breakfast instead. Blake ordered the same, and they dug into biscuits and gravy, ham and bacon, scrambled eggs, two sides of toast, hash browns, and even the strawberry and cantaloupe garnish.

"Lord, you two have healthy appetites," their waitress said as she poured coffee into their white mugs. "You boys need anything else?"

"No. Thank you." Beau glanced up from his

plate and noticed the many sets of eyes on him and his brother. He and Blake were used to scrutiny, as if people where trying to see the slight differences in their faces. He glanced around as he chewed. It was still unnerving. Especially since they sat at a table in the middle of the restaurant and could be viewed a full three-sixty. "I forgot how much people stare."

Blake shoved some toast into his mouth and looked up. He chewed and washed it down with coffee. "I don't think it's so much us as your passenger of the past week. I'm sure they're just dying to ask about Sadie's sister."

Beau returned his attention to his biscuits. "I just dropped her off last night."

"Small town, and the JH employs a lot of people." Blake set his coffee on the table.

"Well, this must be your brother," a voice that rattled like an Abrams tank spoke from the aisle. Beau looked up at an older lady with a pile of gray hair and a stack of wrinkles. She had little cowboy boots dangling from her ears and a white T-shirt with an assault rifle on the front with the words "Come and Take It" written beneath.

"Hello, Luraleen." Blake stood and offered his hand.

"Oh you." She wrapped her skinny arms around Blake's chest. "You know I'm a hugger."

Blake grinned. "That I do." He raised one hand toward Beau, who put down his fork and rose.

223

"Beau, this is Vince's aunt, Luraleen Jinks."

"It's a pleasure, Ms. Jinks." He held out his hand, only to have her wrap around him like a scrawny octopus.

"Call me Luraleen," she said, and gratefully dropped her arms. "You boys go on ahead and sit. I don't want to keep you from your breakfast. The Wild Coyote makes a real good biscuit on Wednesday on account of that Russian Ralf cooking in the kitchen." She looked around and added out of the corner of her mouth. "Never come on the weekends. Friday through Sunday mornings Sarah Louise Baynard-Conseco is in the kitchen. Her biscuits are tough as Texas clay. Probably on account of her husband being currently incarcerated in San Quentin and her not having any man at home to cook for." Then she added as if they'd asked, "Murder."

Beau cut his eyes to his brother, who just shrugged a shoulder. "I'll remember that, Ms. Jinks. It was a pleasure to meet you." He put a hand on the table to take his seat, but she wasn't done, and he had to remain standing.

"And of course, you just brung Clive Hollowell's illegitimate daughter to town to finally meet Sadie Jo." Her blue eyes drilled into Beau as if she expected him to speak. He kept quiet but she did not return the favor. "Isn't that just a scandal? Who would have thought?" She shook her head. "Did you get to know her pretty good? All those days alone? Just you and her? I forgot that girl's name. What did you say it was?"

"I didn't, Ms. Jinks." Beau softened the news with a smile. "I can't tell you anything. If you want to know about Sadie's sister, you'll have to talk to Sadie."

Luraleen's eyes got squinty. "That girl never says nothing to nobody. Thinks she's too good for her raisins." She finally shuffled off. "Deserted her poor daddy for all those years," she mumbled.

The brothers sat and Blake picked up his coffee. "That Luraleen is a pistol."

Beau reached for his fork. "A crazy pistol with a loose trigger."

"She's okay. I got to know her a bit when I was helping Vince." He picked up his fork and shoveled a few bites of eggs into his mouth. Did Beau look like that when he ate? What had Stella called him? *A healthy eater?* "What did you and Sadie's little sister do?" Blake asked, and gave a deep amused chuckle. "All those days alone in a car. Just you and her?"

In the car? "Nothing much. I got some business done and she listened to music."

"What kind of business? Are you still on the wagon?"

This was Blake. Beau had to be careful. What he and Stella had done was *no one's* business. "Why do you care?"

"It's not natural." He paused for the waitress

to refill their coffee and move away before he added, "It makes a man crazy and mean."

"What's your excuse?"

"Forgot my brain bucket a time or two in Afghanistan." He looked up and was only half kidding. "Don't tell Mom," he said.

Beau seriously doubted his brother forgot his helmet. He would no more leave the wire without his brain bucket than without an ample supply of water. "Mom's Facebook friending my old girlfriends." Beau took a drink of his coffee, relieved that Blake had dropped the subject of Stella. "Which means she's contacting your old girlfriends, too."

Blake nodded. "Mimi Van Hinkle gave Mom her phone number and wanted me to call."

"I don't remember Mimi Van Hinkle."

"Tenth grade. Long blond hair and huge boobs for a sixteen-year-old."

"Oh yeah. Her brother had that Kawasaki you stole—"

"Borrowed."

"—borrowed and caught on fire."

Blake grinned. "The tailpipe got too hot and set the nonregulation seat on fire." He chuckled. "I bailed just before it blew to Jesus. Kawasaki down."

"Frag out."

They looked at each other and laughed like they were sixteen again. Like the only two in on a private joke that no one could possibly understand. Like they were best friends.

And it felt good.

Morning sun splashed across the hardwood floors and area rugs, and bathed Stella in white. She stood in front of the window, robe wrapped around her body and sunglasses protecting her eyes from the stabbing light. She held a cell phone in her hand, her thumb skimming for messages, voice mails, and missed calls. There were three but none from Beau.

Why hadn't he called? He'd said he had her back. Where was he? She looked in her contact list for his number and paused with her thumb over his name. Maybe he'd gotten really busy with his brother. Or maybe he thought she was busy with Sadie and was waiting for her to call him. She wanted to talk to him about her night and his. She wanted to call him, even if it was just to hear his voice.

She pressed end instead. She didn't want to chase him. She'd already coerced him into a physical relationship with her. Okay, yeah, he'd kissed her twice, but he wouldn't have taken it further if she hadn't talked him into it. If she hadn't had to get practically naked in front of him on the balcony above Bourbon Street, they wouldn't have ended up in bed that night. Or last night, either. She'd never had to talk a man into fooling around. Never seduced him into it. Why Beau?

Beyond his obvious good looks and six-pack abs, she didn't know. She hadn't really liked him at first. She wasn't quite sure when that had changed. Maybe somewhere between Tampa and Biloxi. It didn't matter now. Because *now* she liked him a whole lot.

She pressed the phone against her lips and pushed aside a panel of the sheer curtains. Several horses roamed around in a corral and barn across the yard while cows in the distance . . . Well, did whatever it was that cows did.

Now that she'd met Sadie, what next? She didn't have a job or an apartment. She felt like she'd just cleared the last hurdle in a race that had started a week ago. What was she going to do now? Texas had always been the goal, the finish line. Where was she going next? She thought of Beau, but of course he wasn't the answer to her problems. For a woman who'd taken care of herself for ten years now, it was surprising how fast she'd come to rely on him.

She heard steps behind her and turned to see her sister looking a bit haggard in blue boxers and a "Lovett or Leave It" T-shirt.

Sadie saw Stella's sunglasses and laughed. "How's your head feeling?"

"Like I drank too much tequila."

"Me too." Sadie sat on the end of the bed

and grabbed the ornate iron frame. "Sorry."

"Don't be sorry. I'm twenty-eight."

"Your first day here, and I lead you astray." Her blue eyes looked into Stella's, and Stella still couldn't believe she was here at the JH. "I feel like I've failed in my big sister duty."

"Well, you haven't been a big sister very long."

"I'd planned to take you for a nice lunch and then a massage at my favorite spa in Amarillo. Really impress you, but I am surely draggin'. Do you mind too much if we stay home today?"

"Not at all." Stella sat on the bed next to her sister. "You can show me around here, if you'd like."

Sadie nodded. "This used to be my bedroom." She ran a hand across the iron frame. "This was Great-Grandmother's bed, and I spent a lot of time in this room as a kid. A lot of time alone."

"Didn't you have friends?" Stella joked.

Sadie nodded. "Sure, but they all lived in town." She crawled across the bed, laid her head on the pillow, and stretched out her long, tan legs. "Town is a long way if you're ten and all you have is a Schwinn."

Stella straightened the covers and put her sunglasses on the nightstand. "What did you do for fun?"

"Sheep." Sadie yawned. "I raised sheep and cows for 4–H. I couldn't wait to get out of Lovett. When I turned eighteen, I left and I never really came back."

Stella spread out next to Sadie. Was she really lying next to her sister? Feeling comfortable enough to confess, "I always thought you must be perfect because our father loved you. I thought living here with him, you must have had the perfect life." *We think we want what we never had,* Sadie had said.

"No. I loved Daddy, but he didn't know what to do with me once my mama died. I ran wild until he'd remember that he had a daughter, a *girl,* and then he'd send me to charm school or drag a piano teacher out here or make the Parton sisters teach me how to cook and do laundry." She rolled her head on the pillow and looked at Stella. "I could shoot and spit straight. Muck out stalls in the morning and serve finger sandwiches and tea on Mama's Wedgwood that afternoon." She smiled. "I was really confused about what I wanted to be when I grew up. It took me a long time to figure it out."

Stella had always thought her sister had her act together. Born knowing her place in the world. "How long?"

Sadie grinned. "Thirty years."

They had that in common and Stella felt comfortable enough to so say, "I always feel like everyone has some sort of plan but me." But not comfortable enough to tell her about Carlos and Vegas, though. Maybe someday. "I've just always worked. If I don't like the job, I find a different one. I'm twenty-eight. I need a plan. A goal." Yeah, she needed to figure it out.

"I spent a lot of time and Daddy's money going to college. I went to four in four different states, and it wasn't until I was thirty that I figured out I wanted to sell houses. It cost me about a thousand bucks and one hundred and sixty-four hours. I loved it. I loved being top seller at the brokerage and kicking butt on people who thought they were better because they'd been selling longer. Or were older." She looked up at the ceiling and smiled. "Men."

Stella laughed. "Male bartenders think they are sooo much better than woman bartenders. The only thing they're better at is lifting kegs of beer or crates of liquor."

"You're a late bloomer like me," Sadie said through another yawn. "You have a few years to figure out your life."

Like me. She'd spent twenty-eight years thinking her sister was smarter, surer, and taller. Well, she clearly was taller but not surer. Were they really alike? It was the old environment versus genetics question. Stella had spent twenty-eight years thinking her sister was one way when she was . . . asleep?

"Sadie?" she whispered. Instead of an answer, Sadie turned on her side and showed Stella the back of her blond head. Stella reached across the pillows and touched her sister's hair, and the sunny highlights woven throughout. They were both so different. Tall. Short. Light. Dark. Raised in not only different states, but different worlds. Yet . . . they had things in common, too.

Stella pulled her hand away. She never thought she'd meet Sadie and had stopped thinking of her until the night Beau had appeared in Ricky's parking lot looking like a ninja/spy.

Seven days. She turned onto her back and her eyes slid shut. Seven days ago she'd thought her life had been blown apart, and she supposed it had.

Perhaps for the better. If nothing else, she'd met her sister and a six-foot Marine who made her feel things she'd never felt before. He made her heart feel all warm and her skin all tingly. He made her feel safe and gave her courage when she'd always relied on her own strength.

It wasn't until she felt a hand on her shoulder, shaking her awake, that she realized she'd fallen asleep.

"Stella, come downstairs and eat something."

Her eyes fluttered open and for several confused moments, she thought she was in a hotel room with Beau.

"Come downstairs and eat," Sadie said. "The boys are all here to shoot skeet."

"Boys?"

"Vince and Blake and Beau."

She was at the JH with her sister. "What time is it?"

"Three."

Stella sat up. "In the afternoon?"

Sadie laughed. "You've been out for a while. Probably the tequila."

That and the past seven days, added to the last two nights when she'd slept very little.

Quickly, Stella showered and dressed in the jeans skirt and blue plaid shirt she'd found in New Orleans. She matched them with her blue panties and matching bra and her jeweled flip-flops. She put on some mascara and lipstick, and with her hair still damp, she moved past the old portraits hanging in the hall and down the front stairs to the entrance.

Beau stood in the living room in front of the fireplace, and her heart and feet stopped at the sight of him. The light from the antler chandelier shone on his strong profile and blond hair. He stared up at the horse painting and looked so handsome and sure—so *man*—that she couldn't believe she'd ever found skinny guys with Mohawks and eyeliner in the least attractive. He wore a black T-shirt and beige cargo pants and his big watch around his wrist.

"I'm glad you're here," she said as she walked into the room. "You left without saying good-bye."

He looked across his shoulder at her, his gray eyes taking her in from her head to her toes, warming every place they touched. "Sorry."

"Did you miss me?"

He smiled. "Of course, honey."

Honey? He'd never called her honey before. She liked Boots better. "I missed you last night," she said just above a whisper.

He turned to face her and took her hand into his warm grasp. His deep voice lowered. "What did you miss most?"

"Your mouth sliding south to my—" She stopped as he raised her hand and kissed her knuckles. There was something different about the gray eyes looking back at her. She couldn't put her finger on it, but his face looked a bit fuller. A scar dented his chin and she pulled her hand away. "You're not Beau."

He shook his head. "Blake Junger, and you must be Stella."

Lord, had she just said something about Beau's mouth sliding south? To his brother? The resemblance to Beau was spooky and raised the hair on her arms. Like when one of Abuela's woo-woo predictions came true. "Yes."

"No wonder he doesn't want to talk about you."

Except for the scar and the indefinable something about the eyes, they were a carbon copy from their blond haircuts to the sound of their voices.

"You're as beautiful as your sister, Sadie."

"Thank you." She smiled up at him. "And you're as handsome as your brother." Probably more charming, too, but his voice didn't make her all tingly like Beau.

"Stella," Beau said to her as he entered the room. "Sadie is looking for you. She made sandwiches."

She turned toward him and didn't even try to hide her smile. "I'm starving."

His gray eyes looked her over much like his brother had, but instead of a little warm feeling, every place his gaze touched caught fire. "I see you've met my brother."

She glanced from one to the other. It was kind of like a science fiction movie about clones. They were even dressed alike. Freaky. "Beau tells me he's the good twin. Is he?"

"Depends." Blake shrugged one big shoulder and raised his gaze to his brother. "Good at what?"

The two stared at each other, the loaded question hanging in the air. Neither spoke, and it was as if they had some sort of twin telepathy. The air grew thick with testosterone and Stella joked to break the man-tension, "So, if I hit one of you, does the other feel it?"

They both turned their attention to her. "No," Beau answered.

"Hold up." Blake raised a hand, palm out. "We've never tested it. Why don't you go ahead and kick my brother in the balls and if I double over, you know I felt it."

She expected Beau to say something equally

rude. Instead the boys chuckled like Blake was really funny. And Beau thought she had a weird sense of humor?

"Vince said you and Sadie had a few tequila shots last night." Beau changed the subject from his balls.

"Too many."

The corners of his lips dipped in an upside-down sympathetic smile and his smooth voice slid down her spine. "Are you hungover, Boots?"

"Not anymore." Down her spine to the backs of her knees. "Slept it off."

"Boots?" Blake's brow wrinkled. "Are you a new recruit?"

"She cycled out," Beau answered for her.

Stella didn't know what that meant and didn't care. Not when she felt all tingly.

"Obviously not."

Beau's upside-down smile turned into a real frown. "Let it go."

Blake shook his head and the tension settled between the two of them again. Only stronger this time. "It wasn't all business and music."

Beau pointed at his brother, then to himself. "You and I aren't going to talk about it."

"It's like that?"

Like what? What was it like? Were they speaking in super-secret twin code?

"Yeah," Beau answered. "It's like that."

Chapter Thirteen

"Pull!"

Stella gave the nylon rope a hard tug and two neon-orange clay pigeons sailed through the air. To her left, Beau raised the barrel of a gun and fired. The shot cracked the air and Stella flinched as a pigeon shattered. In one fluid move, he pulled the pump handle and a spent red shell flew out of the side of the gun. He shot again, and the second pigeon broke apart and fell to the dry ground and prairie grass. Stella flinched once more, but at least she didn't scream this time.

"Good shot," Vince congratulated him.

Beau grinned and handed Sadie's fiancé the gun. "I got a toolbox full of mad skills."

Yes. Yes he did. Stella could attest to some of those skills.

"You winged it," Blake said, and raised a can of Lone Star to his lips.

"Mortally wounded counts."

Stella turned to her job and pulled back the arm of the flinger thing. She bent over to load two orange clay pigeons in the machine, and the shadow from the straw cowboy hat she'd borrowed from Sadie slid down her chin, shading her face from the evening sun. Before they'd all headed out for the skeet field, she'd changed out of her flip-flops and into her old black boots. Sadie had offered her shoes, but Sadie's feet were a size and a half bigger than Stella's.

"Pull!"

Stella yanked the rope and looked over at the shooters about twenty feet away. Vince and Blake watched the sky and shattering orange clay while Sadie stood at a table covered in ammo and kept score in a notebook. The evening sun shone on the concho band around Sadie's cowboy hat and settled in the blond braid hanging down her back.

Sadie had wisely volunteered as scorekeeper rather than participate against three highly competitive special ops warriors.

From behind mirrored sunglasses, she felt Beau watching her. His features were stony, giving nothing away. Since he and Blake had shared some sort of twin telepathy beneath the antler chandelier, he'd grown . . . she didn't know. Distant, maybe.

They'd all laughed and talked while they'd eaten in the kitchen, but even as Beau joked around, she felt the change. She felt it as they grabbed coolers filled with beer and water and drove the half mile to the skeet field hidden from the view of the house by a windbreak of elm and cottonwood. It felt as if they were nothing more than casual friends. As if they hadn't kissed and touched each other—all over. As if he hadn't reached for her hand or held her while she freaked out on the side of a Louisiana highway. As if they hadn't grown close.

Okay, maybe he didn't know her favorite color, and maybe she didn't know his favorite food, but she knew him. She felt connected to him. More connected than she'd ever felt toward another man. She trusted him. Felt like she could sink into him and stay there. The rest was just conversation.

He moved toward her, fluid and smooth, and reached into the cooler on his way.

"You look hot," he said, and handed her the bottle of water.

"Thank you." She wished she could see his eyes. See what he was feeling. See if his eyes were a smoldering gray like he was thinking she was sexy hot or just temperature hot.

"It sounds like everything went okay last night."

She took a drink and lowered the bottle. "What I can recall."

He reached a hand toward her and brushed a drop of water from her bottom lip.

She felt the brush of his finger in her belly and heart. The heat of his touch made her gasp.

"Stella." She didn't need to see his eyes. Want smoldered in the hush of his voice.

"I missed you last night."

"Shhh." He softly pressed his finger to her lips. "Not now." He dropped his hand. "Not here."

She wanted to ask him why and where and when. She wanted to know when he was leaving

Texas. The thought made her feel a little panicky, but he was right. Here and now wasn't the place.

"Do you have a plan for what's next?"

"Dinner. Sadie's cook left something called Texas campfire casserole in the oven."

"No." He smiled and shook his head. "Where are you going after Texas?"

With you. The thought jumped into her head. Unexpected but not shocking. It made no sense but felt logical. Right. She wanted to go wherever he was going. She had money. She could get a job. She swallowed past the lump in her chest. "I'm not sure. Where are you going?"

"Home. I'm thinking of sticking around Nevada for a while. Not travel so much."

"Why?" She bit her bottom lip.

"Tired of the road."

"Oh." She hadn't realized that she'd hoped to hear an altogether different answer until the clog in her throat made her chest ache. "Oh, yeah." She bent down and grabbed two orange targets. "You've been on the road a long time." She was falling in love with him. Falling fast with nothing to hang on to because the one stable thing in her life stood before her talking about a life without her.

"You're up, gyrene," Vince said.

Beau chuckled and turned away. "What's the score?"

"You're still on top. Blake and I are tied."

Stella watched Beau walk away as she loaded the flinger. Her gaze wandered down the back of his wide neck and shoulders. His big arms strained the soft cotton of his sleeves, and the black T-shirt hugged his back and flat waistline. Her gaze got caught on the back pockets of his cargo pants and the bulge of his wallet. He had a good backside. Hard, smooth, almost as good as his front side.

"I'm heading back to warm up dinner," Sadie announced, and placed the pen and notebook on the table next to boxes of shotgun shells. "Do you want to come with me and make the salad, Stella?"

Stella turned her attention to her sister. "Sure," she answered when she would much rather stay and watch Beau's behind. "What do I have to do?"

"Open a bag of lettuce and dump it in a bowl. With your knife skills, maybe cut up a few veggies."

"I can manage that."

"Twenty minutes, Vince," Sadie warned, and looked at her watch. "Dinner will be ready at seven-thirty."

"We'll be there."

Sadie and Stella walked down the short path overgrown with weeds toward the row of elms and cottonwood. "If I don't give them a time limit, they'll be at it all night. Two Navy SEALs against a Marine. No way they'll let him win."

Stella and Sadie jumped in Vince's black truck parked next to the Escalade and headed the half mile to the house. "I can't imagine Beau losing at anything," Stella said. "He's so . . ."

Sadie glanced over and looked at her through gold-tinted sunglasses. "So what?"

"Capable." She glanced out her window at the barn and the horses in the corral. "He seems so good at everything he does." Everything from getting her safely out of her apartment in Miami to fooling around in a Dallas hotel.

"How well did you get to know each other?" Sadie asked as she parked the truck by the back of the house.

Stella thought about her answer while the two of them walked the short distance to the back door. She didn't want to say too much, but she didn't want to sound like she was hiding something, either. "I like him." Their boots thumped across the hardwood of the kitchen and Stella tossed her hat on the kitchen table. Her feelings were so new, a tangle of love and uncertainty knotting her stomach, and she didn't know what to do with them. It was awful and wonderful and terrifying. "He's a good guy."

"If he wasn't, Vince wouldn't have asked him to do us a favor and find you."

Her feet slowed as Sadie moved to the oven and turned it on. Stella had forgotten that detail. Beau had been doing a favor by bringing her to

Texas. He hadn't wanted to, but the funny thing was, it didn't change anything. Didn't bother her. She'd had to practically force the man into a physical relationship. He'd said he broke his rules with her. He'd mixed business and pleasure, and she knew him well enough to know that *did* bother him.

She made the salad while Sadie buttered several loaves of French bread. She watched the clock on the stove and listened to her sister talk about the pregnant mare in the barn. Maribell was due to give birth any day and Sadie hoped for a black-and-white Tobiano. The unborn foal was the last of Clive's breeding endeavors. While Sadie talked about their father's love of paint horses, Stella thought about Beau and wondered how much breaking his rules bothered him and what it meant. She wasn't sure, and the uncertainty put her on edge.

As Stella cut the last cherry tomato, seven-thirty came and went. She was anxious to see Beau's face. His unreadable face that told of tight control and holding back, the tempest in his eyes the only sign of his battle with restraint.

"I knew skeet wasn't a good idea today," Sadie said as she put the foil-wrapped bread in the oven. "But they all promised they wouldn't get super competitive."

Stella cut up a green pepper next, and at seven forty-five the back door opened and Vince stepped inside. "Sorry I'm late." He smiled all cheery and moved to the sink. "I'm starving."

Stella and Sadie looked at each other and then at the closed back door.

"Smells good." He pumped soap into his hands.

"Where are Blake and Beau?" Sadie asked the back of his head.

"Still shooting."

Stella reached for the towel next to the cutting board and brushed green pepper seeds from her fingers. "Still? It's getting late."

"They'll be at it for a while. Better eat without them."

Something was definitely up. Vince's nonchalance was too forced and Beau never passed up a chance to eat. She moved toward the back door to take a look outside.

Vince turned off the water. "You're not thinking of going out there?" The way he said it sounded more like a statement than a question.

Well, she hadn't been thinking about it until now. "Yep. Can I borrow your keys, Sadie?"

"Sure."

"No." Vince stuck up a wet hand. "That's not a good idea."

"Why?" Stella and Sadie asked at the same time.

"They're working out a few things."

"What things?" Stella folded her arms beneath her breasts and waited.

"They're having a discussion." He reached

for a towel on the counter and dried his hands.

Something Beau's mother said popped into Stella's brain. Something about ruining Christmas brunch. "Are they discussing Batman and Superman?"

Vince's eyes cut to her, and for one brief second, his nonchalance slipped and she saw his concern. "Not yet."

"Great." She dropped her arms and headed for the door.

"I'll drive." Sadie followed close behind.

Vince grabbed the keys. "I'll drive."

The few minutes it took to drive the half mile to the skeet field felt more like half an hour. As soon as Stella opened the truck's door, she heard male voices. Not loud like they were shouting at each other, but very clear.

"I can shoot a round through a fly's ass at three hundred meters, you shit-for-brains jarhead."

"Correction, whiskey delta. *Could* shoot. Now you can't hit an elephant's ass with an AT4 launcher."

Stella walked from the crop of trees and her attention immediately landed on the brothers standing about a hundred yards away. They stood practically nose to nose and it was difficult to tell them apart. Thank God they weren't holding any weapons.

"I'm going to shove that fucking HOG's tooth up your ass."

"You're going to try, pudgy fucker, but that's all you're going to do." Beau planted his hands on his brother's chest and forced him to take a step back. "You're drunk and you've gone to fat."

Stella picked up her pace. She sensed rather than saw Sadie and Vince at her side.

Blake shoved back. "And you walk around like you're better than everyone else. Like your dick is special and you're saving your hard-ons for some higher purpose. It's bullshit. You banged Sadie's sister the first chance—"

Beau slammed his fist into Blake's jaw. "I told you not to talk about her."

Blake's head rocked back and he returned the favor with a right jab. "You say you don't want to be like Dad. At least he isn't a hypocrite."

Stella took off toward Beau but Vince's strong grasp on her arm swung her around. "Best just to let them go at it until they knock each other out."

She looked into Vince's face, then back over her shoulder. He was probably right. "I don't think so." She pulled her arm free and ran toward the two pissed-off trained snipers. "What the heck are you two doing?" she shouted as loud as she could.

Beau slammed his fist into his brother's jaw. Blake grabbed him around his neck and they both went down, sounding a lot like two tree stumps hitting the ground.

"I'm nothing like that son of a bitch." They

wrestled in the dirt and weeds and somehow Beau ended up on top, sitting on Blake's chest with his brother's T-shirt wadded up in one fist.

"Stop it!" she yelled as she halted several feet away.

Without taking his eyes from Blake, Beau said through gritted teeth, "Go back to the house, Stella."

She moved closer. "Only if you come with me."

"Listen to your little girlfriend, Beau. Run back to the house, you pussy."

Her fingers felt tingly and she shook her hands. "Don't make me get physical."

They both turned their heads and looked at her, ripped shirts and bloodied lips, identical handsome faces, staring at her like *she* was the one who'd lost *her* mind. She pointed at Beau. "Get off your brother." They both continued to stare at her and she tried not to hyperventilate. "Don't make me call your mom."

"What?"

"Did she just say she was calling Mom?"

"Yes I did." She tried to swallow but her throat was suddenly very dry. "And I will, too."

"Breathe, Boots."

She took as deep a breath as possible and blew it out. "I'm sure Naomi will have something to say about you two hitting each other."

Of all things, Blake smiled. "Your woman is going to tattle?"

Beau of course frowned. "That's what she says."

"And for the record, fighting over who is the toughest superhero is so stupid. Everyone knows the Invisible Woman kicks ass." She didn't know where that had come from or really even what she was talking about. She'd seen Jessica Alba in *Fantastic Four*, and Invisible Woman was the only superheroine that came to mind. She took a few more breaths and added, "She has super powers, becomes invisible, and has cute gloves."

"You two are ri-fucking-diculous," Vince said as he stopped next to Stella. "You've ruined Sadie's dinner party."

Beau looked at the faces above him, then turned his attention to his brother. "Keep your Batcave shut, asshole." He stood and wiped the side of his mouth with the back of his hand. "Sorry about your party, Sadie."

Vince offered Blake a hand and pulled him to his feet. "Yeah," the other twin said, and spit on the ground to his left. "Sorry my brother's a dickhead and ruined your party."

Beau looked at his brother as if he couldn't stand the sight of him. "Drink until your liver explodes. Puke your guts up and drown in your own vomit. I don't give a shit. I'm out of here." He grabbed Stella's hand and pulled her behind him. "Thanks for your hospitality, Sadie. Sorry again about your dinner."

His tight grasp about cut off her circulation and there was no way she could pull free. Good thing she didn't want to pull free.

"Are you okay?" Sadie asked, looking a bit stunned and worried.

"Yes." Stella glanced up at Beau as she practically ran to keep up with him. "Where are we going?"

"Somewhere else."

Stella turned and waved to her sister with her free hand. "I guess I'll see you later." She glanced up at the man who pulled her along. He was filthy. His black T-shirt was dusted with dirt and weeds. "You're pulling my arm off."

"You're lucky I'm just pulling it off and not beating you with the stump," he said as they walked through the trees. "Don't ever do that again, Stella."

"You want to beat me with my stumpy arm? Why? What did I do?" Gee, why was *he* so mad at her and why did she think he was funny?

"Don't get between me and my brother." They stopped by the passenger side of the Escalade and he opened the door.

Okay. Now he wasn't funny. She'd never been the kind of woman to take orders from a man. "Is that your way of telling me to mind my own business?"

"That's my way of telling you that you could have gotten hurt." Anger pinched the corners of his eyes and ran through the steel in his voice. "I didn't see you until we were on the ground. I could have hurt you. Copy that?"

She slid her gaze across his handsome face and stopped on blood at the corner of his lips. "I'm never going to be okay with someone hitting you, Beau." She raised a hand and brushed the slight stubble of his cheek. "Copy *that?*"

One side of his mouth lifted and he visibly relaxed. "Roger, Boots. I copy that."

Chapter Fourteen

He was in too deep. Downrange in unfamiliar territory. His life was starting to feel like a soup sandwich, thanks to the woman walking up the stairs in front of him. The scuff of her boots on concrete was the only sound between them. The ride to Vince's apartment had mostly been silent, with him in deep contemplation about the past half hour. About losing control and hitting his brother. Sure, they'd fought before, but never when one of them was sober. He'd been the sober one. The one whose judgment wasn't fogged by booze, yet he'd thrown the first punch. Blake had opened his mouth about Stella, and Beau had popped him as if there'd been no other option.

"Right here," he said, and reached around in

front of her. The smell of her hair filled his nose and head as he unlocked the door. A picture of his fingers tangled in her hair as she took him into her mouth flashed in his brain. When it came to Stella, it seemed his judgment was fogged and his options MIA.

He shut the door behind him and stared at the back of her blue plaid shirt. She'd been quiet. *Unusually* quiet today. He'd never grabbed a woman and dragged her off like a caveman before. He didn't blame her if she was angry about that. He wasn't real happy with his behavior, either.

She hadn't objected, but that didn't mean she was pleased about getting hauled off in front of her sister. A sister she'd been so worried about impressing. "Stella." He took a step and stopped. What could he say when he didn't know what was going on in his head and hadn't a clue what was going on in that beautiful head of hers? "Should I be sorry I dragged you off?"

She turned and looked at him over her shoulder, her blue eyes matching some of the blue in her shirt. "Are you?"

He should be. He should be sorry about a lot of things. "No."

"No." She shook her head. "I wasn't all that excited to eat something called a Texas campfire casserole anyway." A slow seductive smile tipped her red lips and he felt it in his groin like a white-hot caress. "I'm kind of picky about what I put in my mouth."

The caress in his groin turned to a punch. It knocked the wind from his lungs, and he didn't know who moved first. Him. Her. It didn't matter. He caught her up as she wrapped her legs around his waist.

"I missed you last night." She dropped kisses on his face and lips. "Am I hurting you?"

"No." His laughter turned into a deep groan. "Stella. I'm dirty."

"I like you dirty." She ran her fingers through his hair as her warm breath touched his jaw and the side of his neck. "I like it when you forget you're perfect. When you forget about doing the right thing and get dirty with me."

"Stella." His lips found hers and his hands worked the buttons of her shirt until it was open. He pushed it down her arms, and his tongue slid into her warm, wet mouth. The feeding kiss turned up passion, and against the front of his pants, she pressed her crotch into his erection. It felt so good it hurt. A fire flash of pain and pleasure that turned him as hard as Burma teak and sent a rush of desire through his veins. Throbbing want and need and greed pounded his groin and made him single-minded. Focused on the woman wrapped around his waist. He unhooked her bra and tossed it behind him. Her plump breasts filled his hands. Her pink nipples poked his palms and made him think of all the things he was going to do to her. All the places he was going to kiss her. All the places she was going to kiss him. All the inventive things he would do so that he didn't slide his erection into her hot, luscious peach. All the different positions he'd use to keep himself from sinking into the ultimate pleasure. Even in his lust-saturated brain, he knew that was not an option. Not for her. Not for him.

Stella unhooked her feet from around Beau's waist and stood. She pulled off his shirt and kissed his neck and chest as she shoved one hand down the front of his pants. "Mmm," she moaned as she wrapped her palm around his silky steel erection. She loved the feel of him in her hand and the taste of his skin against her tongue. She sucked on his neck and bit his flesh as she shoved his underwear and pants down his legs. His penis jutted from his body and brushed her belly above the waistband of her shorts. Hot and smooth, and she stepped back far enough to look at the clear bead resting in the middle of the plump head.

"I like the beast," she said, and smeared the sticky drop on her skin.

"The beast likes you." He removed her hand and kissed her knuckles. "Too much." He took a few steps back and sat on the couch. His gaze touched her mouth and breasts and belly as he took off his boots. "Drop your pants, little girl."

Her hands slid across her stomach to her zipper. "I'm not a little girl." Her shorts dropped to her boots, then she kicked them to the side.

"No. You're not." Once completely naked, he sat back against the couch. "You're a beautiful woman."

She moved to stand between his knees. "You think I'm beautiful?" He was beautiful. His hard chest and arms and legs, his erection rising from his dark blond pubic hair. His stiff penis lay against his flat belly; the engorged tip touched his navel.

"Very." His gray eyes smoldered and burned and he leaned forward to bury his face in her abdomen. Her breath caught and burned and he pushed her panties down her legs. He slid one hand between her thighs and she stepped out of her underwear. "You're soft." He kissed the underside of her breast and stroked her sensitive flesh. "And wet."

Her knees buckled, and she straddled him before she fell. Her legs and boots rested on the outsides of his legs and his hands slid to her waist. She looked at his lap so close to her. At his sex and hers and their flat stomachs and naked thighs. Desire brushed across her skin like a hot whisper. A whisper filled with lust and longing and love that singed her flesh. She ached for him all over, in her thighs and breasts and heart. She looked into his sleepy eyes, and her heart pinched and pounded as she rose onto her knees and took his face into her hands. The tip of her breast touched the crease of his lips and his lusty gaze locked with hers as he sucked her into his mouth. The warm tip of his erection brushed the inside of her right thigh. She loved the things he did to her body. Loved how he made her feel and how her heart pounded at his touch. She loved him. Loved him so much it felt like it might burst from her chest.

She reached between them and wrapped her hand around his thick shaft. He pulled back and looked up at her, his gray eyes drugged with lust. "Stand up and open your legs for me." His wet tongue circled her nipple before he added, "There are still a few positions we haven't tried."

Stella had a better idea. She lowered her mouth to his and poured all the love in her heart into the kiss. Her heart grew bigger, her lust burned hotter, and she wanted more.

She wanted to make love to him.

She looked into his face, locking her eyes with his, and sat. The first brush of his penis against her sensitive flesh made her shiver. The first blunt stab made her suck in a breath.

"Stella." His hot gaze widened and his grasp on her waist tightened. "What are you doing?"

She lowered herself a bit more, sliding down another inch. "I want you, Beau. I want to be with you."

"Jesus." He sucked a breath between his teeth. "You gotta stop."

He felt foreign inside her. A little uncomfortable, but she kept going.

His head fell back and his nostrils flared. His fingers pressed into her waist but he didn't move. "I can't stop you."

"I don't want you to stop me." She slid down a bit more.

He swallowed hard and put his hands on her thighs. Gently, he pressed her downward until she was completely impaled. She didn't feel pain, but she wasn't exactly comfortable. Like shoving her size six foot in a size five shoe. More like a pinch than pain.

His hands slid to her back and he pulled her against his bare chest. His arms shook and he buried his face in the crook of her neck. "Stella." He exhaled and sucked in oxygen like he found it difficult to breathe. "Stella. What have you done?"

She'd given him her heart and soul and body and she wasn't sorry. But . . . her own pleasure was quickly being replaced by the tender pinch and her own awkwardness. It had to get better at some point. It had to feel good or people wouldn't do it. "Does it usually feel like this?"

"No." His lips brushed the side of her throat. "Never this good."

"I don't really know what to do now," she confessed.

"I do." With her still clutched against his chest, he changed positions until she lay on her back on the couch with him above her. "Am I hurting you?" He lightly pressed his forehead into hers. "You're tight. I don't want to hurt you, Boots."

Instead of answering, she kissed him and wrapped her legs around his waist. Slowly, he pulled out, then pushed deep inside. The bulbous head of his penis rubbed her slick vaginal walls and awakened a different passion than she'd ever felt before. It built deep inside and got hotter with each long stroke. A deep groan tore from his chest and wrapped around her heart. She was a novice but a fast learner and matched his rhythm of pleasure.

His harsh, warm breath brushed her face as he drove into her faster, deeper, more intense. Pushing into her. Pushing her toward climax. Coaxing a cry from her lungs and a confession from her heart. "I love you, Beau. Oh my God, I love you. Don't stop."

"No stopping now. You feel good. So good," he said through a groan as he thrust into her faster, higher, and hotter. "So soft and slick and so fucking good." He drove his hard penis into her over and over until she hit a peak more intense than she'd ever felt before. Scalding heat constricted her inner muscles and spread fire outward across her body. He held her face in his hands as he plunged deeper. Her climax spread, hotter, burning more intense.

"Come for me, Stella." His body surrounded hers, covering her in warmth and pleasure, and as always, she felt protected. "You're beautiful."

Her toes inside her boots curled and she cried out at the new and exquisite pleasure of him deep inside her. The pleasure of giving herself to the man she loved.

The muscles in his arms and chest turned to stone. His breath whooshed from his lungs and he swore like a Marine. In and out, a smooth pump of his hips until his breathing finally slowed and he stopped. He dropped his face into her neck and asked, "Did I hurt you?"

"No." She did feel a bit raw, but so content she didn't care. "Are you okay?"

"I'm better than okay. I love watching your eyes when you come." He kissed her nose. "That was so good, Stella."

It was better than good. There just weren't words to describe how good it felt to be with him. Like this. She was twenty-eight. She'd been a grown woman for a long time. She didn't need a man to make her a woman, but Beau made her feel complete. Gave her something she'd never known before. "Can we do that some more?"

"Are you sure you're up to it?"

"Oh yeah."

"Then we're going to do that all night long."

And they did, stopping around midnight to take a shower, and he made dinner of frozen pizza and cheese sticks they found in the freezer.

"How was your first time?" he asked, but the cocky, knowing grin twisting his mouth told her he knew the answer.

"Better than . . ." She thought a moment of all the possibilities that she could compare it to: sparklers and infernos and warm fluffy clouds. Of all the possibilities he would understand. "Better than flashbang."

"Better?" He chuckled. "It's damn near impossible to top a good flashbang."

She smiled. "Yet somehow you managed." Which wasn't surprising. Beau was good at most things. Perfect. "Your flashbang is wonderful." There was one thing that could have made last night perfect: if he told her he loved her. He had to love her, she told herself as he took her hand and took her back to bed. She could not feel so overwhelmed, so overpowered by her love for Beau and him feel nothing. It was too big to be felt by her alone.

He had to love her. She felt it in the way he looked at her and kissed the side of her neck. The way he touched her was different than it had been when they'd just fooled around. It lingered a fraction longer as if he didn't want to stop. He'd made love to her, but he never told her he loved her. Not even when she curled against him and felt his soft kiss on her shoulder as she fell asleep.

Beau sat on the couch in his black boxers and listened to the voice on the other end of his phone. He stared at his bare toes and said, "I thought you might talk to Blake before I confront him."

"What makes you think he'll listen to me?" his father asked.

"I don't know that he will, but he needs to talk to someone." God knew he'd tried, but Blake wasn't listening to him these days.

"The guys get benefits and career counseling months before separation from the teams."

"He needs more than a job." All branches offered spec ops counseling before separation, but some guys needed more. "He's drinking himself to death."

"Nah . . . He's just finding his land legs. He's a SEAL. He's faced worse than life as a civie."

"I think he might have PTSD." Beau had hired some vets with PTSD. Worked around some of their issues and knew some of the signs.

"Bullshit! He's a goddamn SEAL sniper with eighty confirmed kills. Not many men have more than your brother."

And they were all aware that Beau had seventy-two. "It wasn't a competition." Not between him and his twin. Every kill shot saved the lives of U.S. and coalition military personnel as well as innocent civilians. They'd both done their job, but they hadn't been in competition about the targets they'd removed. "I'm not asking you to agree with me or admit that Blake might need the kind of help he isn't getting from a bottle."

"He'll work it out." William Junger had never suffered from post-traumatic stress, therefore it was a weak man's excuse. Beau's own transition from the military had been fairly smooth, but that didn't mean his brother didn't have issues. They had identical DNA, but different fingerprints. They were two different men. "You can't expect a Rottweiler to act like a poodle."

Beau hung his head. He didn't know why he'd called the old man thinking he might be of some help. Maybe because *he* could use a bit of help. Something he hated to admit, even to himself. From "womb to tomb" was more than just something the brothers said to each other. It was their bond created at conception. In good times and bad. A responsibility that lived in their shared souls. Sometimes difficult, but doing the right thing wasn't always easy.

Beau got off the phone with his father and made some calls to a few men he knew in the Veterans Administration. Tension pulled at the back of his neck and tightened his skull. He glanced at his watch and rolled his head from side to side. It was eight a.m., and by the time he got off the phone, a dull ache pulled at the center of his forehead. The master bedroom door opened and he turned as Stella stepped into the hall wearing her blue shirt, little shorts, and boots. Her damp hair curled under her left breast.

Stella. He couldn't let himself get sidetracked by the smile on her lips. Lost in the scent of her throat. Not like every other time she was near. Not like the time he kissed her in the pool and casino. Or when he'd stood on a balcony in New Orleans or last night, when they'd made love, knowing what that meant to her. He could have tried to stop her. Before it had been too late, but he hadn't, knowing what that meant to him. Knowing what he had to do now.

"I used your toothbrush. Considering where you've had your mouth, I didn't think you'd mind."

He could feel her sucking him in, with her smile and blue eyes, and he took a step back. Both physically and mentally. He liked Stella. She was funny and smart and beautiful. "I don't mind." He rubbed his forehead and tossed his phone on the couch and he wished like hell he'd pulled on his pants. He hadn't meant to have this serious conversation in his boxers. "Last night changed everything."

She agreed. She stopped in front of him and folded her arms beneath her breasts. She loved him and that changed everything. Like Colbie Caillat, Beau gave her feelings that she adored.

Tingles that started at her toes and bubbled upward to her stomach and heart. He looked all buff and airbrushed this morning in his boxers. All tight skin and hard muscles, and she was a little sorry she'd bothered to get dressed—until she looked up into his shuttered gray eyes. He held himself tight. Once again hiding behind a stony face.

"We'll get married as soon as I can get a license," he said as if he was ordering a ham sandwich, but with less passion. "Do you want to do it here or Vegas? Vegas would be easier."

"What?" *Married? Easier?* Her arms fell to her sides and shock dropped her jaw. "You want to marry me?" She hadn't even thought that far ahead.

"We have to now."

Have to? Typical, he didn't *ask* her to marry him and he obviously wasn't very happy. "We don't have to do anything."

"I believe we do."

All her tingly feelings started to feel like nauseous bubbles in her stomach. "Because we had sex?" She hadn't been thinking about marriage. Only about how much she loved him. "We don't have to get married, for God's sake." Dinner and a movie would be a good start. "When I said I love you last night, I meant it. I love you, Beau."

He looked at her through his Sergeant Junger

263

gaze and said quite reasonably, "You've known me eight days."

But love wasn't about reason or apparently days on the calendar. "Yes, and I know that I've fallen in love with you. You're my Superman. I feel safe around you. You have my back and I have yours."

"I don't need you to have my back."

"I do anyway." She raised a hand toward him as she felt the first crack in her heart. "You make me feel safe. Like I can do anything. I can stand up to bullies and run through flashbang." She dropped her hand to her side. "I can stand in front of my sister in my father's house with courage and strength."

"You can do those things by yourself. You don't need me."

"I know, but I want you." The crack in her heart spread a little more and she placed a hand over the tumble in her stomach. Confusion spun her head around. He asked her to marry him because of last night? Wait. Wrong . . . he *told* her to marry him because of last night. She loved him and could easily see herself spending the rest of her life with him, but there was only one question really. She swallowed and could barely get it out. She didn't want to know. She had to know. "Do you love me, Beau?"

He folded his arms over his bare chest, retreating even further. "I care about you."

Oh God. She loved him so much it consumed her heart and soul, and she felt sick inside. "I care about stray dogs and cats but I don't want to marry them. Do you love me, Beau? The kind of love that makes your heart ache all over? Like you can't keep it all in? Like it's too big?" She lifted her arms wide, then dropped them to her sides. The backs of her eyes stung and she blinked back her tears. "I love you. I chose to have sex with you because I love you."

His brows lowered over the tempest in his eyes but his voice remained calm, reasonable when he said, "You didn't give me a choice, Stella. You didn't give me time to think of the responsibility."

Responsibility. He felt an obligation to marry her. She'd worked hard not to be any man's obligation and his words hurt worse than if he'd hit her. As if his hog's tooth pierced her chest. "Responsibility," she choked past the stab to her heart. The weight of her pain pressed the breath from her body. "Oh." She tried to breathe and not to cry and breathe. Her eyes stung and her chest hurt. "Okay." She headed past him to the door.

"Where in the hell do you think you're going?" He reached for her and missed.

Away. Away from him. Fast, before she fell apart and he felt responsible to put her back together again. "I don't need you. Remember?" She opened the door and stepped out into the

265

morning light. The sun burned her eyes and she quickly moved down the concrete steps.

"Stella! Get back here."

She stopped by the front of a maroon minivan. The woman loading kids in the vehicle blurred as the first tear spilled from her lower lid. She turned and looked up the steps at Beau, standing at the top in his black underwear. "Get your pants on." She turned and headed in the opposite direction from the Escalade. She moved around the side of the building and sat on the steps leading to another complex. Her hands tingled, her ears rang, and she thought for sure she was going to pass out. She shook her hands and put her head between her knees. She breathed in and out as she stared at a black gum spot on the concrete. A tear splashed on the ground next to the gum. Oh God. She didn't know what to do. She was stuck in a town where she knew no one. No one besides the man who'd just shot her heart. No one but Sadie.

Two more tears dropped to the concrete as she concentrated on her breathing and options. She couldn't fall apart now. On the steps of the Casa Bella Apartment Complex in Lovett, Texas. She sat up and brushed her cheeks. She had to think. She didn't have time for tears. She'd been in bad positions before. With Carlos in Vegas. Singing on a stage while brawls broke out. Getting grabbed by Ricky and pursued by the Gallos. This felt worse than all those times. Crying in a stairwell, her heart shattered, was a lot worse then getting hit in the head with a flying bottle. Several more tears ran down her cheeks and she brushed them aside. She didn't have her phone or ID or cash or credit cards. Her backpack was at the JH. With Sadie.

Sadie. Even if she had her cell phone, she didn't have her sister's number. Beau did. She rose and rubbed her shoulder against her face. He was the last person she wanted to see right now, and she'd rather chew off her arm than knock on his door. She might not have a choice though. She retraced her steps to the front of the complex and looked around. Beau's Escalade was gone, which was somewhat a relief.

The pregnant woman closed the back hatch of the van and waddled to the driver's side door.

"Excuse me," Stella called to her, and brushed her face with the back of her arm. "Do you have a cell phone I could use for just one call?"

The woman watched her approach and opened the driver's side door to dump her enormous cowhide purse inside. She looked across the parking lot, then back at Stella. "Your man tore out of here in a hurry."

He wasn't her man.

The woman smiled and pulled the phone out of her purse. "He'd put his pants on, though."

Stella managed half a smile. "Thank you so much," she said, and called 411. Sadie had a cell phone but the ranch had a landline. She'd seen it in the kitchen.

"Verizon 411. What city and state?" the operator asked.

"Lovett, Texas."

"What listing?"

"JH Ranch."

"Just a moment."

The pregnant woman rubbed her big belly. "You headed to the JH?"

Stella wasn't sure she wanted to give out that information to a stranger. Not even one who looked as if she was about to give birth on the sidewalk.

"I can give you a ride. I'm on my way to my in-laws about ten miles past."

"Oh, I don't want to put you out."

"It's on the way." She waved away Stella's concern. "I've known Sadie forever. We went all through school together. Lord, we were on the dance squad at Lovett High. The Beaverettes. What a time we had."

The operator came back on the line. "Connecting. Thank you for using Verizon."

"Her daddy just died a few months back, poor thing." The woman shook her head. "I just saw her at the Gas and Go last week. She looked good."

The phone rang once and went to voice mail. Great. Someone was using it. She hung up and handed back the cell.

"I'm RayNetta Colbert."

Stella looked into RayNetta Colbert's brown eyes. The woman had three little kids strapped in her minivan and was so pregnant she could hardly walk. "Are you sure it won't be a bother?" Normally Stella wouldn't even consider a ride from a stranger. But today was anything but normal and what torturous thing could the woman possibly do? Make Stella babysit?

"No bother."

"Thank you," she said, and moved around to the passenger side. She opened the door and sat on a blue M&M stuck to the beige faux-leather seat. "I'm Stella Leon." It still sounded so strange to say it out loud. "Sadie's sister."

RayNetta grinned like she'd just won the Texas lotto and started the van. "Well shit fire and save matches! Welcome to Lovett."

Chapter Fifteen

"Maybe it's Stockholm syndrome."

Stella looked at her sister in the pedicure chair next to her. "Maybe, except I wasn't kidnapped and held captive." It had been two days since she'd run from Beau. Two days of confusion and self-recriminations. Two days of every emotional pain imaginable.

"He phoned Vince this morning."

The pedicurist inside Lily Belle Salon and Spa in Amarillo scrubbed Stella's heel with a pumice stone. Stella wasn't surprised Beau had called. He'd called her phone four times in the past few days. She didn't answer and he didn't leave a message. "He feels responsible for me."

"Maybe." Sadie giggled as a second pedicurist sanded her feet. "God that tickles."

The pumice stone did tickle a bit, but not like Sadie carried on. Watching her sister squirm and laugh brought a smile to Stella's lips.

"He obviously has feelings for you," Sadie managed.

Feelings. He cared. It wasn't love and it wasn't enough. After the pedicure, they drove to Lovett and bought glittery cowgirl belts at Deeann's Duds. That was the first time they heard the latest gossip flying around town. The wild story about Blake's twin brother chasing Sadie's long-lost sister from his apartment wearing nothing but black boxers.

"That is true," she confessed to her sister on their drive to the JH. "But he chased *after* me. He didn't chase me *from* the apartment." She wasn't used to strangers talking about her. Knowing her embarrassing business. It was bad enough that Sadie knew, but it got worse. A day later they heard a version where Beau had been naked.

"I'm sorry," Sadie said as they exited the Albertson's, where a checker had relayed the latest.

"No. I'm sorry to bring so much drama."

Sadie shrugged. "Everyone in town loves gossip. It was bound to happen."

That night she heard a third version as she sat in the barn next to Sadie petting Maribell's forehead as the mare gave birth. Vince stood at the other end next to the vet and said, "Velma Patterson came into the store today and said you were seen running from my apartment building wearing nothing but army boots and a camo bandana."

"I was naked?"

Vince shrugged. "I wouldn't have mentioned it, but I thought you should know."

"Next they'll say you parachuted in with a knife between your teeth." Sadie sighed. "The truth is never quite colorful enough."

Maribell's nostrils flared and the big animal groaned.

"Holy shit!" Vince swore as he knelt by the vet. "I see a foot."

"You'll see one hoof and then the other," the vet said as he worked on the business end. After several more pushes, Maribell delivered a gray and white filly. She was beautiful and perfect, and Sadie openly cried as she knelt by the foal, the last link to her father. "She's beautiful, Daddy."

Stella bent down by her sister and put an arm around her shoulder. "I've never seen anything like that," she said as tears clouded her vision.

"I'll never forget tonight." Stella and Sadie sobbed while Vince cleared his throat and stared suspiciously off at nothing. "It was truly a miracle. A treasure to see."

Sadie nodded and wiped her nose on the back of her sleeve. "She is a treasure. I was going to name her Cadeau because it means gift and sounds fancy, but I think Tesoro fits her better. Or is it Tesora?"

Stella smiled. "Tesora." The moment was perfect. A perfect, joyous moment with her sister. But amid all the joy and tears, her broken heart reminded her that her life was less than perfect. She loved a man who didn't love her. She was homeless and jobless and the small town of Lovett thought she ran around naked in combat boots and a camo do-rag. That night, she lay in bed and thought about her life. She had a few ideas about what she wanted to do next and she ran them through her brain. Mostly she thought of Beau. His laughter and rare smiles. His strength and his touch and the emotionless look in his eyes when he said she was a responsibility.

She'd wanted him to be the first man to make love to her. She didn't regret it. She loved him and he'd made her first time so good for her. Her only regret was that he felt the need to marry her out of obligation. Not love. Thinking back on it, she guessed she shouldn't have been surprised. Beau always tried to do the right thing even if it wasn't right for him. Now, five days later, that still felt like a blow to the chest.

She swallowed past the pain in her heart. Someday, when she started dating again, it was back to skinny boys with black fingernail polish and eyeliner. No chance of her falling for those guys. At least not so hard. Not completely and totally in love.

The next morning as Stella and Sadie checked up on Tesora a business envelope arrived for Stella. No letter. No quick message. Just a set of keys and the address to a storage locker in Miami. Beau really didn't plan to come back. He really didn't plan to see her. Which was for the best. Her eyes pinched and watered. Even if it felt like the worst.

"I'm thinking of going back to school. Part-time." A sad smile touched her lips as she ran her hand over the filly's soft mane. "Maybe taking a few core classes until I figure things out."

"That sounds like a great idea." Sadie ran a brush down Maribell's side and looked at her over the horse's back. She asked cautiously as if she was preparing herself not to like the answer, "Where were you thinking of enrolling?"

Stella answered just as cautiously, "West Texas A&M."

From across the horse, Sadie's eyes smiled. "In Amarillo?"

"If that's okay with you."

"I'd love that. You can stay here with me."

Stella shook her head. No way was she going be the third wheel at the JH. "I thought I'd get an apartment in town." And a car. The PT Cruiser would never make the trip from Florida to the Texas panhandle. She'd have to sell it.

"No one is staying in Vince's place and his lease isn't up for three more months."

The apartment where she'd given Beau her virginity? "No. Thank you."

"I understand." Sadie cleared her throat. "I'll help you find a nice place."

Tesora bumped Stella's palm with her unbelievably soft nose. "First, I need to fly to Miami."

Sadie's brow wrinkled. "I thought you were afraid of flying."

Oh, that's right. She'd lied about that. A lie that had changed her life and cost her a chunk of her heart. She made a vow to herself not to lie anymore.

She looked down and scratched the foal's forehead. Well, not as much.

"When I see you again, you'll probably be a surfer." Beau raised his hand from the steering wheel of the rented BMW and made the hang loose sign.

"Probably," Blake agreed. "I'll have a long ponytail and zinc oxide on my nose." He pulled a few oranges from a bag of fruit they'd picked up after they'd left the airport that morning. "Probably say 'dude' a lot like Trevor Mattis. Did you ever meet Trevor?"

From behind his sunglasses Beau glanced at his brother and the ocean beyond as they drove down the Pacific Coast Highway toward Malibu. "Nah."

"He was a surfer dude. A real good frogman from Team One, Alpha Platoon. Laid back. Real cool under pressure. The kind of guy you want in the comms center."

Beau turned his attention to the road. He didn't say anything. Just let Blake talk if he felt like it. It had taken him almost a week to get him this far.

"Played everything from Nirvana to Neil Diamond on the guitar." Blake paused and tore at the orange peel. "Until a Toyota packed with explosive rammed his Humvee in Mussayab and took him out. A paratrooper and John Kramer from Delta were killed, too. Along with about twenty-seven civilians just trying to make their annual pilgrimage to Kerbala. Poor bastards." He dropped a large peel on the leg of his jeans. "I heard they had to scoop Trevor up with a spoon." He shoved several orange sections into his mouth. "Does this rehab place have a lap pool?"

"I think they have several." He'd spent the past week sitting on his brother, sometimes physically, at his home in Nevada before Blake had agreed to enter a private rehab in Malibu that specialized in PTSD and substance abuse.

"This whole rehab thing probably won't work," Blake predicted, and hit the switch to roll down the window.

"Give it a try. Who knows? Maybe you'll seduce a hot nurse."

"If there is a hot nurse."

"It's Malibu. I think maybe it's a law."

"Maybe it won't be a total waste," Blake grumbled like he was only going to rehab to please Beau and their mother, but they both knew he wouldn't have gotten his ass on the plane if he wasn't ready for a change. He opened his window and tossed out the orange peels. "Expensive lay, though."

"What are you doing?" Beau looked at his brother, then back at the road. "You just littered."

"Orange peels aren't litter. They're biodegradable material."

"Orange peels lure animals onto the road." His brows slammed together and he couldn't seem to keep himself from adding, "That's how innocent critters get killed."

Blake looked across the car as if Beau had grown fairy wings and sprinkled himself with glitter. "You sound like a girl."

No. He sounded like Stella, and he wasn't even surprised when his twin read his mind and asked, "Have you heard from little Stella?"

"No. She won't answer her phone or return my calls." And he was still semi-pissed at her for running from Vince's apartment. By the time he'd jumped into his clothes, she'd disappeared. He'd spent a good hour driving around with his nuts lodged in his throat looking for her.

"Too bad you let that one get away."

Now it was his turn to look at his brother as if he'd sprouted wings.

"Any woman who wades into a fight to save her man is a keeper." He chewed more orange slices and chuckled. "That was funny as fuck."

Beau frowned. "She could have gotten hurt."

"Yeah, but she didn't." He swallowed and scoffed, "Invisible Woman. Cute gloves. Ridiculous."

Beau scoffed, too. "Can kick Batman's ass."

"And Superman," Blake reminded him.

His laughter died. "Yeah." He didn't need reminding. He felt it every day, and it felt like a five-foot woman had worked him over—kicked his ass. Hard. Twisted his guts and spun his head around. She'd said she loved him. Really loved him. She'd wanted him to be the first man to make love to her. A decision that she more than likely regretted now.

The wind whipping through his brother's window irritated him and he rolled it up. He thought of Stella's face when she'd asked if he loved her. Expectant. Hopeful, almost pleading with him to say yes. He'd almost said it, too. To spare her the pain of his answer. To spare himself the look in her eyes when he said he cared for her.

Blake fooled around with the sunroof, and the smell of ocean air filled the car. In the end, Beau hadn't been able to say what he didn't believe to be true. Wasn't real love supposed to hit like a thirty-eight caliber to the chest plate? Wasn't it supposed to knock a man back and send him to his knees thinking, "What the fuck." Wasn't it a flash and a bang that blew a man apart?

He closed the sunroof. No. It wasn't like flashbang or a round to your armor. It was feeling like you'd been cursed with an annoying woman for eight days. It was confusion and tunnel vision when she was around. Longing when she wasn't that blew a man apart. "Jesus," he whispered.

"What is it?" Blake asked as he busily texted.

Beau turned to his brother. "I might be sick."

"Have an orange." Blake glanced up. "You look like you just got hit on the side of the head with a billy bat."

It felt like it. His chest, too. He looked at his brother. His best friend and comrade from the womb, and heard himself say as if from a long distance, "I love her." How had that happened? How had extreme lust turned to love?

"No shit." Blake snorted and tossed an orange into the cup holder.

And when? When had it happened? When he'd

watched her bravely walk into her sister's house? Or in New Orleans when he'd pretended like he couldn't say no to her? Or before that, under a quarter moon in Tampa when he'd looked up and seen her? The lighted water reflecting in her hair?

What the fuck?

Blake shook his head and it was like looking into a mirror and seeing a disgusted image of himself. "And you're supposed to be the smart twin."

The Ramada Inn just north of the Miami International Airport wasn't exactly the lap of luxury, but neither was it a fleabag. Mostly, it was affordable, and now that Stella was on a tight budget, seventy bucks a night was all she could afford. It was a far cry from the hotels she'd stayed in with Beau, but that had been before. Before she'd fallen in love with a super-secret spy Marine. Before he'd broken her heart.

Stella looked out the window of her second-story hotel room and into the empty parking lot. She was all about looking to the future now. No looking back. Looking back still hurt. The wounds still as fresh as they'd been a week ago.

She'd been in Miami three days and had accomplished a lot. She'd sold her car to the manager of her old apartment complex, and had to admit, going there to get the car had been freaky and a little frightening. She'd half expected the

Gallos or Ricky to jump out at her, but nothing had happened. She guessed they'd given up and moved on. When she met with the complex manager to give him her apartment keys, they'd worked out a fair deal for the Cruiser. She'd been able to pay off the rest of the loan and still have a little cash for a down payment on her next car. Used, of course.

All that was left to do was drive the ten-foot U-Haul she'd rented to her storage shed tomorrow and pack it up. There was a hand truck in the back of the U-Haul, and she figured if she needed more help than that, she could leave the items behind. Anything of real value to her had been boxed up and taped shut by Beau's friends.

Stella moved away from the window and grabbed her phone off the bed. She checked for calls and e-mails and text messages. Nothing. Nothing since the last time she'd checked an hour ago.

Beau hadn't tried to contact her in five days. She'd received nothing from him since the envelope he'd sent in the mail. The jerk-wad. He really hadn't loved her. He'd spun her head and broken her heart and turned her life upside down. He'd made her love him, but he'd never loved her.

I care about you, he'd said, and she'd never felt so foolish. Never. Not even that time she'd streaked through a Tennessee bar, only to realize, once she'd raced outside, that she'd left her clothes back in the women's bathroom. In her own defense, she'd been highly intoxicated and a friend had bet her twenty bucks.

With Beau, she didn't have an excuse. Not money or booze or double-dog dare.

She tossed the phone on the bed as someone knocked on the door with what sounded like a key.

"Housekeeping."

Housekeeping? Most housekeepers were women. This voice clearly belonged to a man, and she quietly moved to the door and looked through the peephole. She half expected to see Lefty Lou, not a pair of gray eyes staring back at her from beneath a Marine baseball cap. Her heart thumped in her chest and ears and she held her breath. Afraid to move. Afraid to make a sound. Afraid to blink and he'd disappear.

"I know you're there, Boots. Open up."

How did he know?

"I'm not going away."

She knew him well enough to believe him. Part of her heart screamed a steady *Yes yes yes!* while the other part yelled, *No no no!* She compromised and opened the door, but she left the guard on just in case. "What are you doing here?"

He moved his face closer to the opening. "The question is, what are *you* doing here? I told you not to come back to Miami."

"Well, I don't take orders from you, Sergeant Junger."

"That's obvious." His familiar frown settled into place as he rocked back on his heels. "Why didn't you answer my phone calls?"

The ones he left five days ago? "That's obvious."

He wore a bright white T-shirt and his usual cargo pants. Her stomach got its usual tight feeling. "What are your plans?" he asked.

God, she hated him. No, she loved him. No, she hated that she loved him. "None of your business."

He tried to smile, like he was all Mr. Friendly, but it didn't reach his eyes. "Humor me, Boots."

Fine, what did it matter? She'd tell him and he'd leave and then she could go pass out from anxiety. "I'm packing up a U-Haul tomorrow and driving to Lovett. I talked to the manager of Slim Clem's and he'll give me a job working nights. And I'm taking a few classes at West Texas A&M in Amarillo this spring."

All pretext of happy smiles vanished. "Slim Clem's is a dive."

"I've worked in worse." Just the sound of his voice stabbed at the wounds in her heart.

"This hotel is a dive. The security isn't worth shit."

"I've stayed in worse, too." She cleared her throat to cover the waver in her voice. "I've got to go now," she said before the tears pinching her eyes blurred her vision and the *yes yes yes* part of her cracked heart won and she threw open the door. "Good-bye, Beau."

He raised a hand. "Stella—"

She slammed the door as her eyes flooded. "Go away before I call the cops." It was an empty threat but it apparently worked. She heard his footsteps, then looked out the peephole. He was gone. He'd just left. The a-hole.

She moved to the bed and the strap of her blue sundress slid down her arm. She couldn't believe he'd left. That easy? Like when he'd left Lovett. One minute he'd been in town and in the next he'd vanished. Like the super-secret spy he assured everyone he wasn't. His brother had left with him, too. Which had been good. The last thing she'd needed was to run into a carbon copy of Beau.

She brushed her tears from her face and rose to check the peephole once more. Yep. He was gone. She turned and leaned her back against the door. If he was just going to leave, why had he come? Why was he here? Why hadn't she asked him?

The hard wood felt cool against her bare shoulders and she wiped away more tears. How had he tracked her down? Sadie and Vince were the only two people who knew where she was, and she doubted her sister would give Beau any info. That left Vince, or else Beau had tracked her cell phone. She closed her eyes and rested her head back against the door. He'd probably tracked her.

A loud bang brought her upright and her eyes wide open. Another loud bang, followed by several big pops, made her jump so hard her spine made a cracking noise. Outside, it sounded like a shootout was going down in the parking lot and she ran to her window. She pushed aside the drapes and stared down at the thick white and gray smoke rising from the lot. For a brief second she thought maybe a car had exploded, then Beau walked through the smoke, arms loose at his sides as he looked up at her window.

"Flashbang," she whispered as he stopped just below and tilted his head back. He'd brought her flashbang.

Another crackle like the Fourth of July sent her racing from the room. She flew out the exterior door and down the steps, toward Beau like she had that day she'd run from two mobsters. Only this time, there was only Beau, standing in front of smoke like he was descending from a cloud. No fancy hearts or flowers. Just flashbang and him.

She stopped ten feet away. Suddenly unsure.

"Someone told me that I give excellent flash-bang."

"I think I said wonderful." The strong smell of sulfur burned her nose and stung her eyes.

He smiled and didn't seem affected at all. Maybe because he loved the smell of flashbang. "Then I'll have to work harder." He closed the distance between them as a few people stuck their heads out of the motel. "I've missed you, Stella."

She tried not to smile or let his words make her think he cared about her. Oh wait, he did *care* about her.

"You've led me on a chase trying to track you down. Vince wouldn't tell me where you were for fear Sadie would gut him."

She folded her arms beneath her breasts as a breeze carried the smoke away. Thank God.

"Aren't you afraid someone will see all this smoke and call the police or fire department?"

He grinned. "I flashed a badge and told the girl working the front desk that I'd be checking out the motel's security. Not to get alarmed if she sees or hears anything unusual."

"Like bombs and smoke?"

His grin got even wider. "Exactly."

She'd rarely seen that grin. Which she had to admit was pretty handsome. "Why are you here?"

His grin faded and his eyes moved across her face. He simply said, "I love you."

Her arms fell to her sides and she was afraid to blink. Afraid this was all a dream. "You said you didn't love me."

"I'm an idiot. I thought love happened like bullets and flashbang." He waved the smoke away. "I was wrong. It happens one smile at a time. One beautiful, torturous smile at a time. One look into your eyes. One touch of your hand. The sound of your laughter." He closed the small distance between them and took her hands in his. "I'm a Marine, and I expected something that was so life-changing as love to slam into my chest and knock me to my knees." He smiled and raised her knuckles to his lips. "Instead it started out soft and small. Sweet. Like you."

Okay. She liked that. That was good. That and the kisses across her fingers. She'd never seen this Beau. She could get used to him.

"Here I am," he said, and ran his hands up her arms to her shoulders. "Slammed in the chest and knocked to my knees. I love you, Estella Immaculata. I want to look into your eyes and feel your touch for the rest of my life. You gave me the best gift I've ever received. You gave me you. Marry me. Not because we had sex and I feel responsible, but because I love you."

Oh God! She couldn't breathe. Her heart grew too big. She was going to faint for sure this time. "It would really suck if you did all this," she said and waved a hand toward the flashbang canisters, "and I said no."

He gave her his best Sergeant Junger look, but a smile creased his eyes. "Your joke isn't funny."

She laughed anyway. "Yes," she answered. "I'll marry you."

He picked her up so that her gaze was level with his. "Promise you won't run from me again like you ran from Vince's apartment."

"I left. I didn't run."

"You scared the shit out of me, is what you did. I drove around looking for you for an hour. If Vince hadn't called me, I'd still be driving around Lovett."

"Never again. Wherever you are, that's where I am. Where I want and need to be." She placed her hands on the sides of his face as the last of the smoke trailed away. "I love you. You're my very own super-duper secret spy." He opened his mouth to correct her and she put a finger softly to his lips. "You are my superhero and I will always run to you."

Center Point Large Print
600 Brooks Road / PO Box 1
Thorndike ME 04986-0001 USA

(207) 568-3717

US & Canada:
1 800 929-9108
www.centerpointlargeprint.com